BONE'S PARADOX

By

BUCK STIENKE

Cover by: Ken R. Farmer

THE AUTHOR

 Buck Stienke is a Texas native from Houston. He moved to the central Texas hill country when he was ten and found the rural lifestyle more to his liking. After graduating from the USAF Academy with a BS in Engineering Management, Buck flew single and multi-engine jets and multi-engine recip aircraft for the Air Force before embarking on a twenty five year commercial airline career. In addition to aviation, his widely varied interests have included ranching, professional football player, gourmet cooking, singer / songwriter, sporting goods retailer, big game hunting, gunsmith, machinist, and designer of suppressors. Each of these interests are reflected in his writings.

DEDICATION

I'd like to thank my wife Carolyn for her forbearance during the writing of this book. I don't have much free time available after normal business hours, and for six weeks this project took many evenings tied to a keyboard.

ISBN-13: 978-1-7329119-5-6
ISBN-10: 1-7329119-5-9
Timber Creek Press
Imprint of Timber Creek Productions, LLC
312 N. Commerce St.
Gainesville, Texas 76240

Published by: Timber Creek Press
timbercreekpresss@yahoo.com
www.timbercreekpress.net
Facebook Book Page:
 www.facebook.com/TimberCreekPress

ACKNOWLEDGMENT

The author gratefully acknowledges Lt. Colonel Clyde DeLoach, USMC (Ret.) and Ken Farmer for their wonderful assistance in editing this book.

TIMBER CREEK PRESS

CHAPTER ONE

COOKE COUNTY COURTHOUSE
GAINESVILLE, TEXAS
WEDNESDAY JULY 15, 2014

The hot July sun had been baking the stone steps for hours when District Judge John Lockhart exited the double doors on the west side of the historic four story brick and concrete building, accompanied by his thirty year old administrative assistant, Cindy

Tanner. "My God, it must be a hundred and five out here," she blurted as the dry southwest breeze tousled her shoulder-length blond hair.

The older attorney chuckled at her comment. "Come on now, darlin'. I know you won't melt before you get to your car. Some people say they even offer air conditioning in the new Lexus models these days."

The two continued down the broad steps and onto the sidewalk on the east side of Commerce Street.

"Very funny, Judge. As the saying goes…don't quit your day job. Hey, big boy…will I see you tonight?" She flashed a dazzling white smile and ran the tip of her tongue across her upper row of teeth. Cindy winked her left eye seductively.

He grinned. "Probably. My wife has some sort of charity event planning meeting this evening. Let's see if I can sneak out for an hour or so."

"I'll be waiting." Cindy spun around on her five inch heels and headed for her red Lexus.

John watched for a couple of seconds as her tight skirt undulated with every step of her shapely, tanned, toned legs. *My, oh, my*, mused Lockhart.

Life is good. He turned and headed for his Lincoln Navigator parked nearby in his reserved spot.

Suddenly, a strange look crossed his face. The silver-haired fifty year old stopped abruptly. His body stood upright, poker straight and began to vibrate—at first, slowly and then, with rapidly increasing frequency and amplitude—as a trickle of blood emerged from his right nostril followed by another much larger one from his left.

The grip of the judge's hand relaxed, dropping his expensive burgundy leather briefcase on the sidewalk with a clatter. His jaw fell open but he could not voice the scream that he wanted to let out. The whites of both eyes turned bright crimson and blood streaked down his tortured face, covering the silken tie and crisp starched shirt that he wore. His knees buckled, and his body fell forward, face down on the scorching hot pavement with a sickening *splatt.*

Cindy had just reached her car when the she heard the noise of his briefcase fall. She turned to look as he stood facing the opposite direction "Judge? Are you okay?" she called out.

As he toppled forward, she let out a piercing shriek, "No! Johnny, no!" She ran up the sidewalk and quickly rolled him over on his back. Cindy gasped and tried not to vomit.

Her startled scream alerted a tall man wearing a Resitol straw cowboy hat on the west side of Commerce Street that had just left Wiese's jewelry store. He raised a hand to stop a slow-moving pickup truck and sprinted across the bricked street to offer aid.

"What happened, miss?"

"I don't know…he was fine ten seconds ago," Cindy sobbed.

He looked at the pool of blood surrounding the head of the injured man and quickly reviewed the first-aid training he had taken in the Army. He knelt down to get a closer look as the instruction came back to him in brief flashes. *Stop the bleeding. No…get the airways clear, chest compressions. Wait a sec. Blood from the eyes? Holy crap! Is that the Ebola virus?* He got back to his feet and fumbled for his cell phone. Frantically, he dialed 911.

BONE'S PARADOX

GAINESVILLE POLICE DEPARTMENT

The on-duty dispatcher, Laurie Williams, was a short, twenty-three year old black woman who was studying part time to get an associate degree in law enforcement. She answered with a cheery voice, "911 Emergency. What city, please?"

"Gainesville! I'm in Gainesville!" came the frantic reply.

"What is the nature of your emergency, sir?"

"There's a man down on the west side of the courthouse. He's bleeding real bad from the nose and eyes."

"Oh, my goodness. I'll send an ambulance right away, sir. Please stay on the line…"

The man gave her his name and address after a few seconds break. Before he finished, he could hear the sound of an ambulance. *What? Oh, yeah, they are only two blocks away, over by the county jail.* He turned to the sobbing woman kneeling next to him.

"It's okay, Ma'am. Help is just around the corner."

WILSON ESTATE
RURAL COOKE COUNTY

Nestled in the rolling hills west of Gainesville, a two hundred acre piece of heaven on earth featured manicured lawns, a lavish ranch style home and barns for the thoroughbred horses the previous owner had raised.

The current owner, Brittany Wilson—a thirty-five year old bombshell who maintained the sexy athletic body that she had displayed during her years as a Dallas Cowboy cheerleader—enjoyed the resort style residential setting. But, she soon tired of the horse breeding operation and sold it off (for a substantial sum of money).

As the sun rose up above the trees east of the house, Brittany, and her boyfriend Christian Ritter, moved out to the lanai surrounding the beautifully landscaped pool.

He carried a pitcher of frozen margaritas and some crystal glasses to an acrylic-topped table set between two lounge chairs.

She settled in to her thickly-padded chair and held out her nicely manicured hand. "No salt for me, but would like a slice of lime on the rim."

"Think that I can remember that little detail." He grinned broadly and he shook his head. "I'm not just a pretty face, you know." He laughed as he poured her drink and set the full circle of a lime slice on the edge of the Waterford. "Here you go, you little palomino."

Brittany took a sip and smiled back at him as she admired his tanned, chiseled body. "No, I must say…there's a lot more to like about you than just your face, but it is such a pretty face, Chris…Don't you think?"

"If you say so." He chuckled. "It got me a lot of work in Dallas, New York, and LA."

She leaned forward and with a snap of her head, tossed her waist-length blond mane in front of her and let it drape down between her breasts and almost to her powder blue thong.

Um-um, Chris thought as he gazed at her lanky body. He moistened his glass rim, dipped it into the saucer of sea salt, and then filled it with a top-shelf frozen margarita. He held it up toward her. "Here's to health, wealth, beauty, and multi-orgasmic sex!"

She grinned. "I love the way you think, you frisky devil." They clinked their drinks together and each took a sip.

Christian set his drink down and reached out his hand. "Come on, why don't we take a little swim?"

She shook her head. "You have any idea how long it takes to dry this hair? Go ahead, I want to be pretty for you…later."

"Have it your way." He set his glass down and turned toward the pool.

Brittany set up with one elbow on the arm rest. "Why don't you show me that dive you are so proud of?"

"Yeah, baby. That half-gainer from a piked position? Prepare to be freakin' amazed." He turned back and gave her a long wet kiss. "This one's for you."

He moved to the one-meter board, stepped up and walked all the way to the end. Flexing both legs, he sprung up, testing the resiliency of the board. Chris bent his legs slightly, and stopped the board's motion when he landed again and then took two steps back. He blew her a kiss and stretched both arms out in front of him as he prepared for his dive. Stepping forward, he pumped his arms down and then rapidly up and he leaped up and landed on the tip of the springboard. His body rocketed skyward with the added force from the diving board.

Chris raised his hands high over head, his feet perfectly pointed downward as his washboard abs contracted and his legs began to rise gracefully toward his body. A look of confusion crossed his face as his mouth flew open. His hands came to his temples as his body began to vibrate and then went limp.

Brittany watched on, confused as her boyfriend fell clumsily into the water, landing flat on his back. "Chris! Chris! What's wrong?" she yelled, scrambled to her feet and raced to the pool's edge. She looked on in horror as his body sank to the bottom, a trail of blood streaming from his nose and mouth. "No! Chris!"

Suddenly, a searing pain hit her abdominal area. She doubled over in agony. The feeling is unlike anything she ever experienced. For a brief moment, it stopped as she caught a ragged breath. Looking at the far edge of the pool area, she saw a figure step from the bushes. A glimmer of recognition crossed her face.

"You!"

She turned to run as another, stronger pain hit her in the side, and then radiated up between the shoulder blades. She coughed, as blood sprayed from her mouth. Brittany fell forward onto her chaise lounge and writhed in misery as she rolled over on her back. Her body convulsed one more time and abruptly became still. Her blue eyes stared sightlessly at the cloudless Texas sky.

NORTH TEXAS MEDICAL CENTER MEDICAL EXAMINER'S OFFICE

Doctor Milton Fisk was well into the autopsy of the former District Judge. He wore his usual daily attire, rainbow Reeboks, a pair of light-blue scrubs on the bottom and a Disney cartoon-print top. His crewcut style hair was still was brown, but thinning at the front. A blood stained white apron completed his work outfit, except when he wore the full face shield or 3.00 readers for close-up details.

He had the chest cavity split wide open, the heart removed and in a glass bowl on one of several digital scales. The deceased person's cranial cap had been detached by a saw cut around the circumference. Fisk peered at the exposed brain for several seconds, and then leaned down and looked at the posterior side of the badly damage organ. "Damnedest thing I ever saw," he muttered. He peeled off his latex gloves and pulled the cell phone from his scrubs.

GAINESVILLE POLICE DEPARTMENT DETECTIVES OFFICE

Detective Darrel Ulysses Bone was seated at his usual desk. Inspector Loraine Rodriquez, a newer addition to the force had a desk across the aisle from his. Both were cluttered with stacks of supplemental reports, the bane of police work.
Bone's cell phone rang with his favorite ring-tone - *La Bamba*. The big man glanced at the caller ID and grinned. "Hey, Doc! Top of the mornin' to you. What can I do for the Prince of Pathology?"

"Morning, big guy. I need you to stop by and look at the results of an autopsy I'm doing on Judge Lockhart. Thought originally it was a simple case of a brain aneurysm, but when I got inside…well, let's just say things got a little weird."

"You don't say?" Bone's eyebrows raised and a sly grin came to his lips. "A little weird is right down my alley."

He glanced over to Loraine to make sure she was tuned in to his conversation. "Tell you what, Doc, these supplementals have about wore out their welcome. I'll grab my sidekick and we'll be right on over. She's a real gas. You'll like her...Laterbye."

Loraine's dark-brown eyes narrowed as she cast a glance his way. "I'll side kick you..."

"No doubt about it. Hey...Ever see an autopsy before?"

"Plenty of times." She looked away as she muttered, "On TV."

"Just as I suspected. Hells bells...First time for everything, Pard. Plus you might even find ol' Doc Fisk kinda charming...in a professional manner, of course."

He tried to suppress his grin, rather unsuccessfully. Bone pushed back his chair and brought his six-foot-eight inch frame to its full height. He pulled a Stetson straw hat off the brass rack mounted on the wall beside his desk. "Grab your gear, grasshopper. We got us a prime opportunity to leave this mundane paper chase behind and maybe do some real police work for a change."

"Why do I get the feeling that we're gonna get ourselves up to our asses in something far worse than a load of paperwork before this day is done?"

She shook her head, and saved the report on her laptop. Once she was satisfied that her last few hours of work were secure, she lowered the screen on her Dell and got to her feet. "Now…I'm almost ready. Just gotta powder my nose." She smiled a fake smile and headed for the lady's room.

§§§

CHAPTER TWO

NORTH GRANDE AVENUE
GAINESVILLE, TEXAS

The black and gold Chevrolet police cruiser was traveling northbound with moderate traffic flow when Dispatcher Laurie's voice crackled over the radio, "Bravo 28, dispatch."

Stella Johnson, the drop dead, gorgeous three year veteran took the call. "Bravo 28, go ahead Laurie."

"Bravo 28, see the woman at the Nothing But Chocolate store at the Gainesville Outlet Mall food court. Abandoned child found on premises."

Stella's partner, rookie patrol officer Juan Gomez glanced over at her as she processed the call. He noted that behind her Ray Ban sunglasses her gold-hued eyes narrowed a bit.

"Bravo 28 is 10-51. ETA 5 minutes." Her voice was notably colder.

"Dispatch copies, your contact name is Gina West. Forwarding it now on your COMMSCREEN."

"10-4, Bravo 28 out." Stella checked both her side and rearview mirrors, and then glanced down at the larger computer flat screen mounted on a swiveling platform between the two officers. "If I get my hands on the POS that abandoned that kid, I'll kick their ass all the way back to the station."

Juan grinned. "I'll hold your hat."

He settled back in his seat and kept a sharp eye on the surrounding traffic and small businesses that lined the major north/south thoroughfare through the town of 16,000. Juan was a clean-cut, small-framed Hispanic who had just finished his bachelor's degree in criminal justice at North Texas University in nearby Denton, Texas. He was happy to have landed a job so quickly after graduation, but eager to start moving up the ladder in his new career.

NORTH TEXAS MEDICAL CENTER

Bone whipped his VW Thing into the single parking spot marked *POLICE USE ONLY* near the emergency room entrance on the west side of the building.

Loraine exited the passenger side and adjusted the Kimber 1911 holstered on her right side. "You know, those seats are really not all that comfortable with hardware on."

"No worse than that Mustang convertible of yours."

"But at least mine has air conditioning," she replied as she pulled her closely tailored white blouse away from her damp spine.

Bone donned his Stetson as he silently admired her hourglass figure. "Got a point there, Pard. But your ride can't match the leg room in mine, not to mention the off-road capability. And my new Porsche engine...runs like a top, don't you think?"

"Yeah, it does. Thought that you'd junk it after those yahoos shot the original VW motor full of holes, but that's not your style...is it?"

Bone chuckled. "I guess you are getting to know me, after all. Thanks to my old buddy, Smith and Wesson here, they won't be shooting at anybody...anymore."

He patted the stainless-steel Model 500 on his right hip. Nestled in a black basket weave leather holster, the massive five shot cylinder was covered completely, but the custom white dog bone inlay on the oversized black finger groove grips was a eye-catcher. Bone had done the art work himself, one of a seemingly endless list of talents he possessed.

Entering through the automatic doors near the ER, they took a right down an adjoining corridor toward the office next door to the pathology lab. Bone took his oversized aviator style Ray Bans off and hung them on the top button of his crisply-starched, white western cut shirt.

"Feels nice in here." Loraine breathed in deeply.

"'Bout sixty eight degrees, I reckon. Keeps infections down is what I'm told."

The two approached a door marked

Medical Examiner

Doctor Milton Fisk

Bone opened the door for his partner. "Last chance to say no, little bit."

"You kidding me? I'm tougher than I look."

"Don't go all kung fu on me, Pard, but you don't look…I mean…you look kinda…"

"Can it, bonehead. We got a job to do," she bristled.

"Yessum."

She entered the room and he followed. She stopped abruptly when her gaze caught sight of the Judge's nude body strapped to a huge stainless steel table with his chest propped wide open and the top of his skull and brain both missing.

Bone bumped into her, only slightly, and then stepped around her to approach the pathologist from behind. The Doctor was seated on a chrome plated stool studying some slides on a large microscope mounted on a table on the far side of the room. Beside him was a metal tray with the blood-covered brain of the deceased. He apparently didn't know the two were even in the room.

"Doc," Bone called out. There was no response. "Hey, Doc," he said a little louder.

When that got no response, Bone moved closer and tapped Fisk on the shoulder. He spun around and grinned, taking two earbuds from his ears. He turned the tiny voice device in his pocket to the off position.

"Sorry, Bone, I was reviewing my description of the autopsy up to this point…Making sure it could make sense to a listener, you know."

"Sound like a reasonable thing to do." He turned back to Loraine and motioned for her to move closer. "Come meet the Doc."

She was somewhat unsteady as she walked the twenty feet across the room. Loraine made sure she didn't take her eyes off the pathologist.

"Loraine, Doctor Milton Fisk, or as I call him, the Prince of Pathology. Doc, this lovely lady is Inspector Loraine Rodriguez, my erstwhile partner."

She extended her hand and smiled, her perfect white teeth glistened in the bright LED lights of the well-lit room. "Pleasure to meet you, Doctor."

"No, Ma'am. The pleasure is all mine, I assure you...Don't get to meet many specimens like you in this line of work."

Loraine blushed, Bone chuckled.

"Don't think she's been called a specimen before, Doc...Have to remember that."

She shot him a look.

"So, Doc, what's the big deal here?" He glanced at the brain and pointed his huge right thumb at it. "You didn't have to make us lunch."

Loraine nailed the big man with a sharp jab to the ribs.

"Ow, Pard. Could have busted rib!"

"If I wanted it broken...it would be." She glared up at him.

Doc Fisk grinned and held up his hands. "All right...settle down children. We have a bit of a problem...At least I think there's a problem."

"What did you do to the brain, Doc? I thought they were supposed to be gray."

Doc nodded. "They are...In fact, I've never seen anything like this that didn't involve a high impact trauma."

"Like a head-on car crash?" asked Loraine.

"Exactly, except in those cases the damage is usually limited to the prefrontal cortex."

Bone and Loraine both nodded.

Doc stepped to one side and pointed at the microscope. "Here you go, Detective. Check out this slide and tell me what you see."

Bone eagerly obliged. He tilted his Stetson back to clear the apparatus and took a seat. Adjusting the eyepieces to focus for his vision, he stared at the amorphous mass of jumbled tiny capillaries—resembling broken spaghetti in a marinara sauce. "Holy crap! All the blood vessels are like...like they exploded...What the hell did that, Doc?"

Fisk shook his head. "Honestly...don't know. There was no sign of external injury. I'm waiting on the toxicology report now, but don't think it's going to give us much. His hemocrit count appeared normal. Witness said he was fine only seconds before he died. That's why I called you...my Duke of Detectives."

Loraine cracked herself up. "Sure that's not Duck of Detectives? Quack, quack."

Bone glanced over his right shoulder. "Thanks so much, Pard...Gotta admit, you got me stumped,

Doc." A sly grin came to his face. He spun around on the stool and looked directly at Loraine. "Hey, Igor. How about it sidekick? You wanna look at the brain at 400 power?"

She shook her head vigorously. "Nope. I haven't had lunch yet...I was wondering about a hemmorhagic agent like the Ebola virus...but it doesn't act that fast does it?"

"No," Doc sighed. "Y'all can be thankful it doesn't...or all three of us would have been dead by now."

"Bummer indeed," Bone replied. "That would ruin the rest of my week...Doc can you email me some copies of those slides? I'll start with runnin' it past some of my contacts to see if any of them ever heard of such a case. You were right...It's more than a little bit weird."

GAINESVILLE OUTLET MALL

Stella and Juan rolled up outside the building housing the food court and parked in the *NO PARKING* zone. They exited the vehicle and made their way into the expansive structure. Spotting a forty year old woman seated with a child that appeared to be around three years old, they approached her. The woman waved.

"You must be Gina West." Stella extended her hand. "I'm Corporal Stella Johnson and this is Patolman Juan Gomez with the GPD."

"Thank you for getting here so soon. I bought her a small Pepsi. She seemed rather thirsty, but I don't know much Spanish...Sorry."

"Don't apologize. You did great. We'll take over from here. If we have further questions, we know where to find you."

Gina nodded. "Bye, sweetie," she said to the young Hispanic girl.

Stella took a seat and asked her, "Does that taste good?"

Her question was greeted with a questioning look.

"*¿Le gusta la cola?*" asked Juan.

"*Si, Señor,*" she replied.

"*¿*Cuál es tu nombre?"

"Mi nombre es Carmen Santiago."

"*Bueno, Carmen. Mi nombre es Juan. ¿Donde esta su madre and padre?*"

Carmen shrugged and simply shook her head.

A concerned look crossed Juan's face. "Stella, I'll see what other info I can coax out of her, if you like to go check with the head of mall security."

"He should have access to all the security tapes as we discussed. First, I think I'll check the lady's room just to make sure her mom didn't have a medical emergency and couldn't hear the PSA. If we can't locate someone from her family in twenty minutes, we'll need to contact Child Protective Services. "

"Gotcha. I'll be Mr. Mom till you get back." He turned to the young girl and spotted a Saint Christopher medal on a tiny gold chain around her neck. *"Esta es una hermosa medallón de San Cristóbal, Carmen."*

She smiled sweetly and replied, *"Gracias, Señor, mi madre me a lo dio a me."*

Stella stood up and walked to the public rest rooms and found the lady's room vacant. *I'm getting a bad feeling about this one.* She left though the food court's south exit, and turned right to the mall general offices.

She introduced herself to Rick Zimmerer, a handsome man in his early 30s—head of Mall Security.

"Pleased to meet you miss. How may I be of service?"

"We have an abandoned child out in the food court. I was wondering of we could review the security footage from earlier this morning?"

"Absolutely. We record it in high def digital format and keep it for 30 days. Should not be too much a problem if you have a few minutes."

Stella flashed a dazzling smile. "That would be wonderful. Gina said that she noticed the child seated by herself a little before 10 AM."

"Great, follow me into my inner sanctum."

Rick walked to a solid metal door and used a magnetic ID badge to gain access at a security panel. He opened the door leading to a 12x6 windowless room. Inside were banks of monitors, a computer and three empty chairs.

"Have a seat, Stella." He pulled out one of the gray leather padded armchairs on rollers and then sat down in an adjacent one. "The food court opens at 9:30 sharp. Let's start scanning those around 9:45."

"Sounds good to me. Can you isolate on the Nothing But Chocolate feed?...The kid was found near there."

"Should be no problem." Rick's hand flew across the keyboard making a series of inputs into the system. "Here we go…There!" He pointed at the monitor directly in front of them—a 36 inch high def flat screen. "This is the feed looking at their register. You can see several tables in the back ground."

"Lets' see what you got."

He started playing the recording, and then moved it to 2x normal and then to 3x speed. Several customers made purchases and they watched people walking by. Then the monitor displayed a man and small child sitting down.

"Stop…Back up a tad…Freeze that!"

The man had his back to the camera, but the child looked like it might be Carmen.

"Can you zoom in?"

"Piece of cake." Rick used a mouse and cursor and built a box around the target couple. He zoomed in to show the child's face clearly.

"Bingo! That's her…The time code is 9:51. Let's see what time he leaves."

"You got it." Rick fast-forwarded the recording and the man departed a minute later . "He's gone at 9:52, headed for the south doors."

"Can you track him to his car?"

"Quite easily, now that we know who and what time we're looking for." Rick tapped in a few more commands and the outside building cameras picked up the image of the man leaving the building. "Gotcha! Now let's see who this jackass is." He zoomed in and the face of the man filled the screen. "There's your man…I assume you want a copy."

Stella felt her pulse quicken as she looked at the person who abandoned his child. "Damn straight I do…Sorry for the language. I get a little bent out of shape when kids are mistreated. Here's a flash drive I carry for times like this." She handed him the small 16 Gig drive and he inserted it in the computer's USB port.

"No need to apologize. Besides, I like women who have some substance to them."

She looked at him and felt her face flush from the obvious compliment. "Rick, do you think that we can follow him to his car?"

"Let's see." He worked the keyboard again and caught the man entering an older light gray Ford Taurus.

He backed up, a crossing traffic of an opposite direction Chevy Tahoe, followed by a Dodge pickup truck obscured the first three letters of the license plate.

"Dammit! All I got is Texas plate number L 436. Can't get a clear view at the first two letters." He turned to her. "Sorry...Best we can do. The other car followed him out of the parking lot and blocked him the whole way. He went south on the I-35 access road...if that's any help."

"You've done plenty. With make model and color, we'll get him...Hey, thanks for all your technical help. If you ever think about joining the PD, I'd be happy to put in a good word for you."

"I'll think about it." He grinned. " I...uh...would like to buy you a drink some time."

Stella returned the smile and fished out a business card from her handbag. "That would be great. But only if I can buy you one first...I owe you. My cell number is on the back." She handed him her card as he smiled like a Cheshire cat.

§§§

CHAPTER THREE

GAINESVILLE POLICE DEPARTMENT

Bone and Loraine were seated at their desks working on the backlog of supplemental reports. Suddenly, a thought crossed his mind. "Hey, Pard, what if the good judge was taking some kind of blood thinner for stroke prevention and he had a high blood pressure spike?"

"Possible...But don't you think Doc Fisk would have seen something like that before? In any event, the toxicology reports would confirm it."

Bone's brow furrowed as his line of thought was shot down in flames. "Guess you're right."

"Hallelujah! Praise be to God! I'll mark my calendar." She dragged her phone out of her purse and pretended to make an entry in it.

"What?"

"You just said that you thought I was right about something."

Bone broke into a huge grin. "Don't let it go to your head, Shortcakes...It would be a good idea to check out his medical records to eliminate that as a causal factor. Think you can find out who his PCP was?"

She crossed her arms. "Duh! I'll just call his secretary. They know everything...One other thing. Why do you call me Shortcakes? For your information, I'm five foot three and a half." She sat erect as if to prove her point.

Bone chuckled. "And a half? Sometimes I don't know if it's easier to jump over you or run around."

BONE'S PARADOX

Loraine bristled and her dark eyes flashed. "Damn you, Bone! Are you insinuating that I'm *fat*?"

He held up both hands in surrender. "No…no. Hell, no! You got a great figure…At least I think so…Never seen you naked…"

"Hold it right there, mister. I've caught you staring at my boobs just about every single day. And then, there's the wise cracks…Always somethin' about my poor bra straps and what a tough job they have…"

"Strictly a scientific observation on my part," he deadpanned.

"Listen, Buster. You are treading on seriously thin ice! Just because you outweigh me by one hundred and fifty pounds…"

"One sixty." Bone propped his elbows on the desk, interlocked his fingers and dropped his chin onto the ersatz bridge he had formed. He faked a cheesy smile and began batting his eyes rapidly.

Loraine took in a deep breath and started to say something, but broke out into a laugh instead. "Stop it! You know damn well that I can't be mad at you when you act so stinkin' goofy!"

"Who would want to be mad at little ol' me?...Listen, Pard, it's lunch time. You up for some Chinese? I'm buyin'"

"Why do you always get to choose?"

"Royalty. Royalty has its prerogatives...I'm the Duke of Detectives."

"Don't let it go to your head, jackalope."

"Then it's time to saddle up and ride," Bone said in his passable imitation of John Wayne.

"Wow...That was good. Pee Wee Hermann, right?" She shot him a fake smile.

GAINESVILLE OUTLET MALL

Bone and Loraine were walking through the food court from the north entrance headed toward a Chinese food concession. Stella entered simultaneously though the south door.

"You'll love the General Tso's Chicken. The Mu Shu Pork is good, too," he said as they approached the counter.

"I thought you were taking me to a real restaurant." Loraine frowned.

"Confucius say *Judge Not Book From Cover*. The same guy owns the Taipei Restaurant on North Grand...Same recipes, shorter wait."

"And Styrofoam plates...Joy to the world."

"Don't be such a stinkin' princess." He noticed Juan seated nearby with a small child. "Hey, let's ask Juan and Stella to join us."

They stepped over to the table with Juan and Carmen just as his partner arrived.

"Hey, guys. Join us for lunch?"

"Thanks for the invite, Bone, but we've got an abandoned child to take to CPS. Ever see this dirt bag before?" Stella handed them a picture of the suspect that Rick had printed.

"Nope...Doesn't ring a bell," Bone replied as he shook his head.

Loraine looked at the print and then at Carmen. "I've seen them at St. Mary's a couple of times last month. The man and his wife were actually kind of private and didn't mix and mingle much. Cute kid...What's her name?"

Juan spoke up. "Carmen Santiago, age three. Doesn't speak English or know where she lives."

"Her father left her here this morning just before 10 o'clock and took off in a white Ford Taurus. I was able to get a partial plate, but missed the first two letters." Stella shrugged.

"Good work, kiddo." Bone gave her a thumbs up. "Run what you've got through TEX DOT and cross with vehicle model and color and you'll narrow the search a lot. Two missing letters leave 676 possible combinations. Make and model knocks the hell out of that."

Juan was incredulous. "How does he know that?"

Loraine grinned and glanced at Bone. "Because he's the Duck of Detectives. Quack."

Bone shook his head. "It's Duke...Son, I've been doing this since you...uh...were a lot younger."

Loraine knelt down beside the young girl and held out her hands. *"Hola, Carmen. Mi llama Loraine."*

She reached out and grabbed onto the policewoman's hands. *"Hola, Señora Loraine. ¿A donde es mi papa?"*

"Nosotros lo buscamos ahora. ¿Es espantado usted?"

She shook her head. *"No. Señor Gomez es conmigo."*

Loraine glanced over at Juan, smiled and nodded, acknowledging his service. *"Todo estará bien. Encontraremos su familia. ¿Está bien una chica grande?"*

Carmen nodded her head in affirmation.

Loraine gave her a big hug as tears fill her eyes. She stood up and looked directly at Stella. "Watch over her. If you need anything, call me."

"You bet," Stella replied as she turned to Juan. "Let's get her downtown and run those leads we've got so far."

Juan took Carmen by the hand as the three headed for the south doors. The little child looked back and waved at Loraine.

The two plainclothes officers were finishing their lunch when Bone's cell phone began to chirp out the strains of *La Bamba*. He flipped the leather protective cover over and caught sight of the caller ID. "Hey, Lauridarlin'. Must be mega important to interrupt my sacred lunch hour."

"Sorry, Bone, but some guy from Philip's Pool Service discovered two dead bodies at the Wilson Estate out on One Horse Lane. Captain St. John wants you two out there ASAP."

"You say frog, and I jump, Lauridarlin'. Laterbye."

Bone closed the leather case and flipped the magnetic locking clasp into position with an audible snap. He dabbed the white paper napkin across his lips and then smiled at his partner as he crumpled the slightly soiled paper into a ball and tossed it onto the last few grains of shrimp fried rice. "Now those were some seriously good groceries...Let's mount up, Tonto."

Bone pulled his VW Thing into the circular drive directly behind the parked GPD patrol unit. He and Loraine exited and headed down the polished granite sidewalk leading to the leaded glass double doors in the main entrance. "Nice crib, Pard, don't you think? Reminds me of my place."

"Sure does. They have walls...And you have walls. They have a roof and..."

"But mine is a corrugated steel roof, of course, instead of slate."

Loraine chuckled. "And not quite 5,000 square feet, like this one."

"But, look at all the money I save on not having a full time maid." Bone grinned and then glanced around at the perfectly maintained shrubbery. "And a full-time landscaping crew." He admired the perfectly shaped half-sphere of a well-trimmed shrub. "*Ilex vomitoria nanna.*"

"What are you babbling about? Your Chinese dinner didn't agree with you?"

"No, you unschooled Philistine. Dwarf Youpon Holly. It's particularly well-suited for our growing climate here in North Texas. By the way...my Five Treasures combo was out friggin' standing. Even the egg rolls and fortune cookie."

"And you just happened to remember the Latin name for holly?"

"Pard, I remember a lot of weird things...Trust me. Sometimes, my mine kinda scares me." His brow furrowed.

"Are you talking about that post cognitive perception thing like when you met Lucy for the first time?"

Bone shook his head. "Not just that one time. We can talk about all that stuff later. Gotta take care of business at hand first."

They stepped up on the raised entryway, flanked by six marble pillars—three on each side. Bone silently admired the workmanship of the lead came in the sidelights. He pressed the doorbell. From some distance away, he could hear the four high—low tones of the chime going off. The two waited for thirty seconds and no one came to the door.

"Hired help must be out in the back." Bone reached for the brass door handle and turned it, swinging the door inside. "Ladies first."

Loraine stepped inside and looked around the inside of a great room, with hugely expensive French furnishings. *Somebody's got good taste.*

Bone followed her inside and took a mental picture of the entire room and it's contents. *Nothing's out of place. Definitely not ransacked.*

They proceeded into a hall, another large room with the furniture facing a north wall. Bone studied the ceiling and spotted the long rectangular cover of a retractable viewing screen. *Nice setup for watching a college football game or old western movie.*

Loraine moved to an exterior glass door and looked outside. "Here's the way out to the back yard. I think the pool is over there." She pointed to the south.

"Lead on, McGruff."

Her dark eyes flashed. "I think the quote is actually *Lay on MacDuff*."

"Of course it is. But it isn't near as funny as McGruff. And I, of course, am not Macbeth, nor do I intend to goad you into mortal combat, o learned Investigator."

"You just love to piss me off…is that it?"

"Oh, Madame Rodriguez, you doth look so very fetching when you have your ire stirred."

"Up yours, Bone." She opened the door. "And you can quote me on that." Loraine stepped outside and closed the door behind her.

Bone chuckled at her and then quickly followed behind. He spotted officer Joel Newman talking to a deeply tanned man in his forties. The man was carrying a water testing kit and wearing a swim suit, tank top and flip flops. His wraparound sunglasses appeared to be Oakleys or a reasonable imitation thereof. Bone's long strides allowed him to get to the perimeter crime scene tape first. He lifted it for his partner and then way over his Stetson and approached the officer. "Okay, Newman…What's the short story, my good man?"

The dark-haired twenty-eight year old patrolman pointed his thumb at the pool cleaner. "Philip Kent here showed up for his regularly scheduled cleaning gig and found Ms. Wilson over there on the chaise." He pointed to the body sprawled out on the lanai. "Spotted the other DB in the pool while he was still on the phone with 911…He's not certain, but he thinks it might be her boyfriend Chris something…doesn't know the guy's last name. I taped off the area and waited for you guys."

"Any signs of a struggle?" Loraine inquired.

Newman shook his head. "Nah…just some dried blood on her lips and chin. Some more over there on the cool deck…but no visible marks on the vic…Kinda weird if you ask me."

Bone and Loraine exchanged glances. Bone slipped a small mirror out of his shirt pocket. He moved slightly to the east of the deceased woman and shined the intense summer sunlight on her open lips and then again to her hands. He studied her facial structure and admired her hour glass figure. *Damn, what a waste of a killer body. She was a somebody's show pony I'm bettin'.*

He checked her well-manicured nails closely. "I think we can rule out robbery as a motive…she's still sporting a $10,000 watch and at least that much in rings."

"Ditto on sexual assault," Loraine added. "She's still wearing her suit."

Bone got to one knee beside the rusty brown-colored dried blood on the pool deck. He lit it up with his mirror and studied it closely. "Interesting," he said to no one in particular. He got back to his feet and moved to the edge of the pool.

The man's body was laying on its back in the deep end. The pool's filtration system had cleared out the liquid blood in the intervening hours since the death occurred.

Bone turned to Joel and Kent. "Philip, you got a long metal pole?"

"Sure...over in the pool house." He spun around and walked to the natural limestone building about 100 feet from the pool itself.

Bone slipped on a pair of latex gloves he kept in a small leather pouch on his belt.

When Philip returned, he handed Bone a long aluminum pole with a double loop of tubing shaped into a shepherd's hook. "Here you go...I assume that this is what you were thinking about."

"Exactly." Bone took the handle and ran the loop all the way to the bottom of the pool. He rotated the tip until it was parallel to the gunnite and slipped it under the dead man's right wrist. With a deft move he lifted the arm and then slid the hook up to the armpit. "Gotcha."

Darrell gently pulled hand over hand on the pole until the body came to the surface.

"Hey, Joel, give a man a hand here."

Each grabbed hold of a wrist and dragged the body over the edge and onto the cool deck.

"Thanks, buddy." Bone glanced at Newman's face. The younger officer was getting a little green at the gills. "You okay?"

"Sure," he lied. "I'm an old hand at this."

"Cool. Just don't hurl at the crime scene...Plays hell with the DNA, you know."

Newman nodded, turned away, and took in a deep breath.

Loraine looked at him knowingly. "It's okay, Joel. You'll be fine."

Bone leaned in closely and noticed the bloodshot whites of the victim's eyes. *Damn. That's the second time I've seen that this week.* He looked over the pool man. "This the boyfriend?"

Philips nodded, his short pony tail bouncing up and down. A sad look crossed his face and his mustache turned into an inverted U shape. "Yessir.

That's him all right…You think he drowned?" He stroked his goatee nervously.

"Too early to say. When's the last time you cleaned the pool?"

"I clean every Tuesday and Friday."

Bone stood up, looked at Loraine, glanced over to the pool, and then once more at the limp body of Brittany Wilson. Turning back to Loraine, he began to rub the back of his head.

Loraine watched the process. *There he goes. Cogitatin' is what he calls it.*

After a few seconds, Bone spoke, "Pard, get a sample of the pool water. I'm thinkin' the vic has been in the water less than 48 hours…not long enough to go into complete rig and not long enough to float. That blood in the sclera is odd. But I bet you a six pack that drowning is not the COD on loverboy here."

"I'll take that bet. I'm thinking the two were out here drinking and he might have hit his head diving into the pool. Could have knocked himself out. Happens all the time."

Bone smiled and walked over to the woman's body. He picked up the pitcher of Margaritas with his gloved hand, sniffed it and set it back down.

"Always a possibility. We'll have Peach run a blood screen on both vics. I also want a sample of the pitcher to test for poisons and bag the glasses. By the way, I like my Shiner Bock really, really cold."

"You're that confidant?"

He shrugged. "Don't have a clue what killed either one of them yet, but I don't think it was liquid. I want to get a couple of good pics of the blood spatter before we swab it…It may or may not belong to the late Ms. Wilson."

Loraine shrugged. "Maybe so, maybe no. You want to do the honors with the pics? Or shall I?

"Oh hell…I better do it. Every time you take pics, you cut the dude's head off."

Loraine laughed. "I guess my secret is out…Subliminal thoughts of repressed anger are likely to show up in the strangest ways." She batted her eyes.

"Don't take a degree in psychology to see that." He fished out his phone and folded the cover back. "Captain Megapixel is here to save the day!"

§§§

CHAPTER FOUR

GAINESVILLE POLICE DEPARTMENT

Stella was at a computer in the common area used by all the patrol officers. Juan walked in alone. She looked up from her data search. "Well, partner, how did it go? Did Carmen freak out when you left her with CPS?"

He took in a deep breath and let it out slowly. "I'll tell you what…that was the hardest thing I've had to do since I got out of the academy. The kid was scared to death and kept asking when they were going to take her home. Just wish I knew where that was."

"I got it down to three white Tauruses in Cooke, Grayson and Denton county with the last four letters and numbers. None unfortunately are registered to anyone with the last name Santiago."

"What if the last owner sold it to him and he simply didn't register it? He's probably here illegally and doesn't have insurance. You can't register without proof of insurance."

Stella smacked the side of her head. "Duh! Why didn't I think of that?"

"Cause I beat you to it. You'd have figured out eventually. Let's print out these leads, We can run their phone listing on the COMMSCREEN en route to St. Mary's. Maybe somebody over there knows where the Santiagos live."

Stella's face brightened as she hit the *print* key. "You know, you might even make a half-decent cop if you keep this up. We're burning daylight…Move your skinny butt!" She snatched up the one page report.

Juan grinned. "Can I drive?"

"No way, Jose."

"Juan. The name is Juan." The newly hired patrolman's face reflected his disappointment.

"You know what they say. 'All you rookies look alike.'"

They both laughed as they headed to the door.

NORTH TEXAS MEDICAL CENTER
MEDICAL EXAMINER'S OFFICE

Chris Ritter's bloody brain was in a stainless steel tray next to the microscope. Loraine tried not to think about it as she peered into the device's eye pieces. The tissue was a complete mess. "Ew...I see what you guys mean. Can't say that I've seen anything like it...Nasty."

Doc Fisk stood a few feet away, with his arms crossed, shaking his head. "Folks, this is indeed a mystery to me. Two victims in two days with identical traumas. This guy should be as healthy as a horse, except for the fact that his brain is utterly destroyed at the capillary level. Damn…its almost like it was microwaved."

Loraine looked up from the microscope. "Doc, any evidence of drowning?"

"Negative. His lungs were clear. The man was dead before he hit the water."

Bone broke into a huge grin. "Shiner Bock…Cold."

Rodriguez shot him a look that would melt steel. She turned back to the pathologist. "So, guess Mister GQ didn't drown…What about his girlfriend?"

Doc Fisk's face clouded up. "Sometimes, I think that I'm losing my touch. I've had three DBs in two days and don't have a clue as to how they came to have massive fatal internal injuries with no external signs of trauma that I can detect."

Bone motioned toward the female body covered with a sheet on the far examining table. "What's her brain look like? Anything like the other two?"

Fisk shook his head vigorously. Nope…no resemblance whatsoever. Her case is entirely different. Ms. Wilson died of a broken heart."

"Say again?"

Fisk managed to make a semi-smile. "Bone, I don't mean that figuratively. I meant it in a literal sense."

"Speak English, Doc. I played football...on a football field...with a football."

The seasoned pathologist walked over to a huge upright refrigerator. He pulled out a container and set it on his desk. Lifting the lid, he displayed the heart of Brittany Wilson. "As you can clearly see, the pericardium was torn. The tear was approximately two centimeters long. Both the left and right subclavian arteries were detached from the aorta with asymmetric tearing consistent with violent traumatic force. The auricles were torn from the ventricles along the auriculo-ventricular groove...Her heart was ripped apart by forces I don't understand."

Bone nodded. "Those type of injuries are more often the result when the driver gets impaled on the steering column in a head-on crash...Right Doc?"

"Sure...even passengers from crashes with seat belts...Princess Diana died that way. But this gal doesn't have a mark on her."

Loraine asked, "What would have caused the blood spatter we found at the scene? It looked projectile."

"The bronchial tubes were ruptured by the same forces that tore her heart apart...On a side note, her pancreas was lacerated badly. The entire thoracic and abdominal cavities were filled with blood...It must have been incredibly painful. Her last breath came out with several CCs of un-oxygenated blood."

Bone shook his head. "What a hell of a way to go. One other thing, Doc. What caused the two male vics eyes to be so bloodshot?"

"Oh, that...The sclerotic covers the choroidal which is highly engorged with small capillaries. It doesn't take much to rupture them, because the are so close to the surface of the eyeball. Any force rapidly applied to the cranium can result in direct contact of the eyeball with the orbital socket, then there you have your hematoma."

"Yeah," Bone agreed. "Seen it in guys who stood too close to tanks or artillery being fired in Operation Iraqi Freedom."

"I didn't know you were in the army."

"Marine Corps, thank you...I was a Captain in Force Recon. Did two tours in Afghanistan. Seems like a long time ago."

Doc nodded. "Anyway, back to these two. Sorry I can't pinpoint the cause of these fatal injuries. If you find the secret, let me know."

Bone reacted to the word *secret*. His body shook a tiny bit and Loraine sensed it.

"You okay? What is it?"

He shook his head. "Not sure...Maybe...Thanks, Doc, you've been a big help."

Bone tilted his head toward the door. "Come on, Double D, let's make some tracks."

"Damn you, Bone!" She backhanded him across the chest. "What did I tell you about calling me that?"

He grinned and stared at her chest for a full two seconds. "You're right. That's not a polite thing to say in mixed company...Besides, they might actually be Double Es. Right Doc?"

Her jaw fell slack. She looked over at Doc Fisk who was unsuccessfully trying to stifle a laugh. Bone had already moved out of range, and she turned a bright shade of red as she stormed after him.

SAINT MARY'S CATHOLIC CHURCH

Sister Mary Elizabeth gazed at the photo Stella showed her. A sad look crossed her face. "Yes, my child, I know this man, Miguel. He's unfortunately not a kind person. Father Joseph has met with him privately, but the Lord has not chosen to answer our prayers...yet. We will continue to pray that God will reach him...but I worry about their marriage."

Juan and Stella nodded. "I know that you cannot divulge the nature of their counseling sessions, but would you happen to know where the couple lives?" asked Juan.

"Permit me to use the computer...Father Joseph insists that we come into the modern age and eliminate file cabinets wherever possible."

"Just like the police department. Everything is going electronic." Stella smiled sweetly.

The middle-aged nun donned a pair of reading glasses and tapped in the first and last name of Lupe Santiago on a Dell keyboard. In a few seconds, the screen switched over to the membership information for the family.

"Here it is…3303 North Buck Street." Just a few blocks from here."

"I know where Buck Street is. Could you print that for me please? I'd hate to remember the wrong address."

"Certainly, young lady. Anything to help get our little girl Carmen home safe and sound." Sister Mary Elizabeth handed the single sheet of paper to the policewoman. "May the Lord bless you and keep you."

Four minutes later, the duo pulled in front of a small, two bedroom, frame house. The front yard was almost brown from lack of summer irrigation. They exited the car and walked quickly to the front porch. Stella knocked on the door. There was no response.

She knocked again, shouting in a loud voice, "Gainesville PD. Open the door!"

Juan got somewhat nervous. "Are you sure this is the house Sister Mary Elizabeth told us about?"

Her golden eyes narrowed. "Yes, I'm sure." She drew her service weapon, a Glock 19, 9mm. "Cover me. I'm goin in."

Juan drew out his Glock 17, and assumed a tactical position beside the door. He felt his pulse quicken. A Ford pickup with twenty-two inch chrome wheels and darkly tinted windows rolled past the Santiago residence. *Dammit. Local drug dealer or gang banger?* The bass tones of a popular Mexican pop tune could be heard as they went by. Juan kept a close eye on it as it turned at the next corner and went east.

Stella grabbed the door handle and turned it—unlocked. She pushed it open wide and took two steps inside, sweeping the meagerly furnished front room for threats. On the simple pine wood end table beside a well worn couch was a family portrait of Carmen and her parents. She kept moving deeper inside the room.

"Clear!"

Juan followed her inside and kept a low tactical position with his 9mm as she walked toe and heel to the short hallway.

She disappeared into the kitchen. He moved to provide cover as she called out, "Clear!"

Juan was breathing faster than normal as he walked through the hall and pushed open the front bedroom door all the way to its stop. He stepped inside as the door bounced off a rubber-tipped door stop and came back almost fully shut.

"Clear!" he called out as he looked at the unmade bed and quickly turned around. The image of a dark clad man holding a gun startled him. He drew the Glock up to eye level and was applying pressure on the trigger when it hit him. "Son of a bitch!"

Stella called out in response to hearing his voice. "Juan?" Her heart raced. She kicked the bedroom door open with her toe. She spotted Juan standing with his weapon at his side, but was primed and ready for any threat. "What?"

Juan shook his head and pointed. "Full-length friggin' mirror! I almost shot my refection."

"Get your head on straight, Rookie." Stella jumped when her radio crackled and startled her, "Bravo 128, dispatch." "Shit," said as she glanced at Juan. She tapped the remote comm microphone on her left shoulder. "Bravo 128, go ahead, Lauri."

"Bravo 128, the suspect vehicle is located at the Santa Fe Railroad Depot. See Officer Newman at that location."

"Bravo 128, roger that. We are 10-51." Stella holstered her weapon and Juan followed suit. She gave him a smirk. "Bet they told you about mirrors in the academy and you promptly forgot all about it."

Juan hung his head. "Guilty as charged, your honor."

"Bet you don't forget again."

"True, that…Hey, partner, I spotted a pic of the family in the living room."

"I saw it, too. We'll grab it on the way out."

SANTA FE RAILROAD DEPOT
GAINESVILLE

Stella pulled up behind the Chevy patrol unit with the overhead lights flashing. Both officers exited the vehicle quickly and approached Joel Newman standing beside the Ford Taurus.

"Hey guys, that was quick. Here's your AP vehicle with the keys still in the ignition."

Stella looked inside. "Have you entered the vehicle?"

"No. I didn't have the background on it…Been tied up all day with multiple DBs. Figured y'all would want to do the field work."

"Yeah, we've been looking for this dirt bag since 10:20 this morning."

Juan walked around the back of the car and bent over, looking at the bumper. A bloody smear was visible on the bumper and a smudged bloody fingerprint was on the trunk. "Oh, crap...Partner, you better look at this!"

She walked to the rear and looked where he was pointing.

Her shoulders slumped. "Aw, Jesus." Stella took a deep breath and let it out slowly. "Newman, can you hand me the keys please."

"You, bet." He flipped open a case on the back of his duty belt and pulled out a single latex glove. Slipping it on, he opened the car door and retrieved the keys.

Meanwhile, Stella wordlessly pulled on a pair of latex gloves and took the keys from her coworker. She inserted the trunk key in the lock. Lifting the trunk, she saw the body of Lupe Santiago with a blanket wrapped around her torso and arms. Blood had seeped though and made an eight-inch rust colored circle around her heart. Stella was shaken by the gruesome sight and turned away. Tears filled her eyes and ran down across her cheeks. "That worthless son of a bitch," she said, sotto voce.

Juan put his hand on her shoulder. "You okay?"

She pulls away from him. "Do I look okay?...Joel, secure the area please. We're gonna go find out if that murdering bastard bought a train ticket."

§§§

CHAPTER FIVE

GAINESVILLE POLICE STATION

Loraine glanced at Bone as they walked from his VW to the back door. "And I still say you are the biggest male chauvinist pig on the planet."

"Really? Cool beans. I was thinkin' about gettin' a personalized license plate that says "Bone #1.""

"It would fit your ego perfectly."

Buck Stienke

"I know...Will you autograph one of your bras for me? Say something like *To the world biggest...*"

"Oh, just bite me, Bone."

"Sounds kinda kinky...I'm all over that."

She tapped her magnetic strip on her ID to gain entry to the *Police Personnel Only* secure door and yanked it open. She slammed it right in Bone's face.

Ooh...Got her really hot this time. Good job. He smiled to himself at his effectiveness in that regard. When he gained access, he didn't turn right to proceed to his own office, rather he cruised left to what the worker bees in the department referred to as the *head shed*. He strode directly to Captain St. John's office, his immediate supervisor and one time Marine Corps commanding officer.

The sturdily built bald black man was seated behind his desk when Bone knocked twice on the metal door frame and entered without being granted permission. St. John glared at the big man as he yanked out a reclining swivel chair, took a seat and put his ostrich skin boots up on the corner of the captain's desk.

"Damn you, Bone...Don't you believe in knockin'?"

"You getting hard of hearin', Cap'n? I knocked twice. Hard." He raised his hand. "Swear on a stack o' Bibles...Listen, I know a killer hearing-aid place. Get you all fixed up...Police discount to boot." He grinned broadly.

"Speaking of boots...off my desk. You were raised in a barn, of that I'm certain."

Bone ignored the directive. "Can you believe this crap? Three DBs in two days...but, beats the hell out of B&Es and penny-ante domestic stuff."

"Not three...Four. Newman just called in with a murder victim in the trunk of a Ford parked down at the depot."

"Ford Taurus? White in color?" Bone's face suddenly took on a serious demeanor.

St. John leaned closer and nodded. "Yeah...How did you hear about it?"

"Dammit to hell...We ran into Stella and Juan during lunch out at the mall. They had picked up a three year old kid who got dumped out there by her old man."

St. John slumped a little. "When it rains it pours...Hey, you didn't come in here because you were lonely or seeking spiritual guidance...What's up?"

"Well, boss...I want to talk to you about my partner."

Loraine was working on her laptop when her desk phone rang. She lifted the hand-piece off the receiver. "Investigator Rodriguez."

"Captain St. John...My office, on the double." The line went dead.

Oh, crap. What have I done now? She wondered. She whipped out her compact makeup mirror and checked herself over. A small touchup on her lipstick and she was mostly satisfied. "This will have to do." Loraine stowed the compact and pushed away from the desk.

She knocked twice on the door frame and stood at attention outside in the hallway.

The older officer motioned to her. "Come in, close the door and have a seat."

Oh, hell. Bone's in here! He's been feeding the Captain a line of bull trying to make me look totally incompetent. And now I have to sit by him. She took a seat in an identical chair like Bone occupied opposite the stern-faced St. John

"Inspector Rodriguez, I've know Detective Bone for more years than I care to remember...We served in the Corps together in Afghanistan, during some really dicey operations, I might add."

Dammit. The good ol' boy network always protects their own asses. She could feel her jaws tighten.

"I've come to trust Bone's judgment in major operational matters...although he often finds a way to try my patience with his cock-eyed sense of humor." He glared at Bone.

"You mean like the time I ran that radio-controlled car covered by a coonskin cap up your leg? Honest, Cap'n. I didn't think that you'd whip out your service pistol and triple tap that little ol' fur cap right here in your office!" Bone chuckled.

"Bone...Stifle yourself." St. John gave him a serious look with a furrowed brow. He then turned to Loraine. "Bone tells me that you have been doing exemplary work this week...helping him get through some emotionally trying cases involving the pathologist lab and multiple homicides."

Loraine nodded and suddenly her face displayed her utter confusion. *Wait...What?*

"Furthermore, he recounted your outstanding work with that abandoned child left at the Outlet

Mall. Young lady, I don't mind telling you that those are the kinds of reports I like to hear about my multitalented professionals in this department." St. John smiled for the first time.

Loraine glanced at Bone, but he would not make eye contact with her.

The captain got to his feet. "I wanted to thank you in person for all you've done. When the promotion board convenes next month, I will be making the recommendation for your promotion to Senior Investigator, based upon merit and Bone's recommendations."

Loraine's jaw dropped. She quickly recovered and stood to shake the captain's hand extended over the desk.

Bone got to his feet. "Congratulations, Shortcakes." Tiny laugh lines around the corners of his eyes gave a hint of his pleasure at the turn of events. He stuck out his right hand, she shook it firmly as her eyes searched his for a clue of what he was truly thinking.

St. John pointed at the door. "All right, people...Enough warm fuzzies for one day. Get your butts to work on those supplemental reports.

Channel 12 called and they're sending over a crew to interview me about the recent series of deaths."

"Hey, boss, I'll handle the press if you like. I know Lisanne personally." Bone smiled at the thought of the gorgeous brunette TV personality holding a microphone up to his face.

"I remember the last time you talked to the press. As I recall, they didn't show a single second of that footage."

"No, Cap'n. I have my secret formula for dealing with the varmints. See, I treat 'em just like mushrooms...Feed 'em bullshit and keep 'em in the dark."

"Out...out. Go on, you two. Get back to work." St. John motioned them to leave and then sank into his black-leather executive chair.

Bone and Loraine walked down the hall in silence, until they passed through the doorway to their own office. Each took a seat at their respective desk.

Loraine looked over at him as he opened his laptop. "Hey, Pard. Can I ask a question?"

He smirked. "Don't you mean...may I ask a question?"

"Yes, dammit. May I ask a question?"

He closed his laptop. "Sure, Pard. Ask me anything."

"What the hell just happened? You've been raggin' on me all week and constantly making snide ass cracks. Then you go into the captain's office and blow enough smoke up his ass till he thinks I'm Dick Tracy or Sherlock friggin' Holmes...How do you explain that?"

Bone laughed out loud. "Okay, little britches, it's like this...I tease you 'cause I like you. You're kinda hot, although way too short for a guy like me. You are real smart. You are capable. You can shoot. You ride a tricked out Indian and drive a Mustang. Your heart is tender as a spring lamb." He coughed into his hand. "But, you're not tough enough for this job...yet...I'm trying...in my own twisted little way to make you a better cop. Just like you push me to be a better detective. You are gonna do great, girl...I believe in you."

Loraine was stunned. "Why didn't you just tell me you thought I was doing a good job?" She shook her head. "I actually thought you and St. John were gonna show me to the door...some macho, Marine, cowboy Mafia bizarro world where women are no damn good."

Bone roared in laughter. "God... you females are so...so sensitive!"

"And you men are too stinkin' macho to just say what's on your mind."

He grinned. "Trust me, you would not like to hear our unfiltered thoughts."

She grinned. "Okay...Maybe so...But, thank you for believing in me."

The big man nodded. "No problem, Pard. Don't let it go to your head." He lifted the cover of his laptop and turned it on. "Couldn't work with a partner with a big head...and big boobs."

SANTA FE TRAIN DEPOT
GAINESVILLE

Stella and Juan approached the sidewalk alongside the 19th century red brick building. Juan glanced at a large silver and black metal plaque marking the building as an official Texas Historic Landmark.

She wiped the tears from her face as she led the way into the passenger terminal section of the building, and moved directly to the ticket counter.

The terminal was basically deserted, and the last passenger train south bound for that night had already departed and the next one northbound to Ardmore and Oklahoma City didn't leave for another two hours.

The two police officers spotted a middle aged local man, Billy Ray Hess working behind the counter. The red-haired car aficionado with black rimmed glasses was reading a copy of Road and Track magazine to while away the time.

Stella spoke first. "Afternoon, sir, Gainesville PD. I wonder if we can ask you a few questions?"

Billy closed the magazine and laid it on the counter. "You bet. Ask away...Get a mite lonely in here some days."

Stella handed the man the photo she took from the Santiago home. "Have you seen this man today...possibly buying a ticket? His name is Miguel Santiago."

Billy studied the picture for a second and then nodded twice. "Oh yeah. One way ticket to Fort Worth connecting on the Texas Eagle to Del Rio, if I remember correctly. I'll check the passenger list for you. Won't take a second." He typed a few words on his keyboard and a list of passengers on the southbound train appeared on his monitor.

Juan leaned in to whisper to Stella. "If he makes it across the border, we'll never see him again. Mexico won't extradite with him facing a possible death penalty."

She locked eyes with the rookie and nodded. "I know."

The agent scanned the list and pointed at the man's name. "I was right…We're not that busy this time of year…not like June vacations, Thanksgiving and Christmas time. That's how come I could remember him. He's not due to arrive until 7:38 tomorrow mornin'."

"Where is that train now?" Juan asked.

"It's not an express…More like a milk run. Stops at every town that had a depot. Let's give it a look see and find out what the full schedule is." He tapped in a few more commands and a new image appeared on his flatscreen monitor.

Billy reached in his shirt pocket and pulled gold pocket watch—the kind you have to wind every day. He flipped open the embossed cover and checked the time. "It's leavin' Temple in eight minutes. Goes through Taylor next. Scheduled to be in Round Rock at 7:40 PM."

Stella took in the information. "Sir, could you print out that schedule for me, please?"

"Shoot fire…No problem at all. Always glad to help." He hit the print button and a few seconds later, the idle printer came to life and spit out a single sheet of paper. " Here, you go, Miss…He do somethn' wrong?"

The simple question hit Stella hard. Visions of Miguel leaving Carmen, killing Lupe and placing her in the trunk of the Taurus flooded in. Tears filled her eyes once more. "Yeah, you could say that."

§§§

CHAPTER SIX

GAINESVILLE POLICE DEPARTMENT

Bone rubbed both eyes. "Can't decide if it's the small fonts or bad lighting in here that's killin' me."

Loraine tried to stifle a yawn. "Paperwork makes the world go round. Or so somebody says...Don't know 'bout you, but I'm about out of gas."

"You up for a beer? I could use a cold one."

"I'll take a rain check, big guy. Haven't forgot I owe you some Shiner Bock."

"Icy cold, preferably."

"Of course. A hot bath and glass of wine are calling." She saved her reports and closed the laptop. "Long day, amigo." She grabbed her purse and moved toward the door.

He grinned. "See you on the other side of midnight." He logged off the PD network and closed up his laptop as well. He grabbed his hat and as an after thought, picked up his laptop. *You never know.*

Bone headed south from Gainesville on highway 51 and quickly found himself in the town of Era, about fifteen miles away. He turned west and hammered down a two lane farm-to-market road toward a even smaller community called Rosston, reportedly the occasional hangout of a famous outlaw named Sam Bass. Cruising through rolling hills dotted with black Angus cattle on the north side of the road and quarter horses grazing on the other, he soon drove up to a twenty-foot wide native stone entryway with a simple metal sign cut out of plate steel held high above by and arched section of heavy 4" drill stem pipe. The sign itself was a play on words—a four foot wide, and ten inch tall representation of a bone. Resembling a Milk Bone dog treat on steroids, it was similar in style to the one inlaid in the handle of his 500 Smith and Wesson duty weapon.

He drove another quarter mile and crested a shallow ridge. To the north, closer to the highly timbered Black Creek near the far property line of his 640 acres, he could see the larger red barn and the nearby house built in 1892. He pulled up in front of a rambling three bedroom dog run style frame home with a three-side wrap-around porch. The ranch house had a new green standing-seam metal roof.

He shut down the Thing. A yellow and white Pit Bull mix dog ran up to the white picket fence surrounding the front yard and started running circles behind the gate. He was wagging his tail vigorously.

"Tyrin, old buddy…Did you miss your old daddy?" It was very obvious from the dog's reaction that he had.

The big guy opened the gate and let the dog out. Tyrin rubbed up against his Wranglers, rolled over on his back and Bone gave him the obligatory belly rub. "Come on, boy, lets get inside where it's a whole lot cooler." Tyrin took off like a shot headed for the door and danced nervously until Bone let him inside.

Bone doffed his Stetson and hung it on a custom built barn-wood and brass hat rack mounted on the wall nearby. "Hey, Lucy, I'm home," Bone hollered in his best Desi Arnaz imitation.

"I heard you when you topped the ridge in that piece of junk you drive," Padrino called out from the kitchen. "In here wonderin' what to fix for dinner."

Bone held up a bag from the local Tom Thumb supermarket. "Brought you some fresh salmon. Wild caught from Alaska...so they say."

Padrino, Bone's 70 year old godfather, a retired Marine Corps Master Gunnery Sergeant, stepped out into the great room. "Just because the heart doc said I need to watch my cholesterol, doesn't mean we have to give up on red meat."

"Never fear, oh wizened wonder. Got us two thick T-bones for Friday and some skirt steaks for fajitas."

"That's more like it...Thought you were goin' full Austin liberal on me for a minute." He grinned.

Bone chuckled. "Just shoot me if that calamity ever happens…How was your day?"

"Good…I took your Cord into Hogan's for an oil change and state safety inspection…Registration was due this month. Had 'em check the generator and battery fluid level while I was there. Runs like a dang thoroughbred. They sure as hell don't make like that anymore."

Bone nodded agreement. "Anything else?"

"Fed the horses and moved the cattle to the east pasture. We could use some rain, you know. How 'bout you? Anything exciting?"

Bone shook his head as he crossed over to the refrigerator. It was a larger 24 cubic foot late model Samsung with double doors up top and a pull-out meat drawer sandwiched below them and the larger freezer drawer below. Set at exactly 31 degrees Fahrenheit, it was that particular feature that sold him on this refrigerator. He laid the salmon and beef in the meat compartment and pulled out a Shiner Bock longneck. He twisted off the cap and drained a third of the nearly frozen bottle in one long gulp.

He ambled back across the great room and sat down in one of two identical oversized burgundy leather recliners. He tugged on the lever on the left side and eased it back. "My day? Man…Weird and weirder…Remember that case I told 'bout yesterday? The judge that had his brain fried to hell and gone out in front of the courthouse?"

"Sure." Padrino took a seat in his own recliner. He crossed his arms over his still flat belly and gazed intently at Bone. "Got it all figured out, do you?"

He shook his head and sighed. "Humpf. Not even close. To top it off, we got two more DBs this afternoon. Similar injuries on the guy, but the chick…now that was a different story."

"How so?"

"Well for starters, the lady's heart was blown to pieces."

"What caliber weapon?"

"Ah ha! Therein lies the rub." Bone held up a single finger. "No entry wounds, no exit wounds. No external bruises or lacerations." He took another sip.

"Dang. That is weird." Padrino wracked his brain to try to relate the events to anything he saw during his stint in the Marine Corps.

Bone grinned. "Believe I already said that."

Padrino sat silent for a few moments. "Any relationship between the victims?"

"Too early to say. The couple we found at the pool wasn't married. The boyfriend was not a local. All I know at this minute is where and when the killings occurred. Who, how and why…now that's a whole different story."

"That's why they pay you the big bucks." Padrino chuckled. "Better start doin' some of that detective stuff, Detective."

Bone killed the last of his beer. He held the empty in his outstretched arm. "Dead soldier…Make yourself useful…while you're up."

Padrino gave him a look. "I'm not up."

"Oh, but you will be when you make yourself useful."

After his second beer, Bone set about making dinner. He set fire to a chimney of charcoal in his Big Green Egg…a heavily constructed hibatchi cooker. Once that minor detail was completed, he opened the package of salmon.

He checked it for remaining bones, but the filleted half had been deboned properly. Without bothering to skin it, he laid it scale side down on a sheet of oiled aluminum foil.

Padrino watched as he made a green salad. "I'm not that fond of skin on my baked fish," he remarked. "The texture is not very appetizing, you know."

Bone spoke like a wizened oriental master he once saw on TV. "Chef say, watch and learn, grasshopper. More than one way to skin venerable cat." He coated the flesh with lemon pepper, a dash of salt and a dab of onion powder. Finally, he squeezed the juice from a single Meyer lemon across the salmon.

Tyrin moved in and began rubbing continuosly on Bone's leg. "Hold your horses, Newt. I know you're a hungry hound...Let me get this fish on the grill first."

He slid the fish and foil onto a wooden platter for transport to the Egg. "It will be ready in ten minutes, amigo. Think you can pan-sear a head of broccoli and finish the salads in that time?"

He gave him a side look once again. "Marines can do anything in 10 minutes."

After ten minutes at 400 degrees in the Egg, the salmon was perfect. Bone reentered the kitchen with the still steaming fish on the platter.

Padrino closed in to the combination island work station and dining table. "Okay, Mister Iron Chef, show me the magic of your new found technique."

Bone took hold of a spatula from a circular tool caddy. He twirled it by the handle as he picked up a dinner plate. "Abracadabra...Let the skin remain on the foil." With a deft hand, he used the sharp blade end to cut off an eight ounce piece of salmon steak and then slipped the blade between the skin and the salmon's flesh. He easily lifted the selected steak off the skin, which stayed firmly stuck to the aluminum.

"I'll be a suck egg mule," Padrino exclaimed. "You know how much time I have wasted trying to skin those damn fish filets in the past?"

Bone nodded as he placed the juicy piece of salmon on his godfather's plate. "Uh huh...Merry Christmas and you're welcome."

§§§

CHAPTER SEVEN

SANTA FE TRAIN DEPOT

Investigator Tye Whittaker dusted the steering wheel for prints after he took the evidence photos he wanted from the trunk and back bumper.

The Cooke County EMS ambulance arrived to transport the victim's body to the county morgue about the same time Juan and Stella returned with the printed train schedule.

Tye directed the ambulance crew to set up the gurney a few feet behind the Ford. "We'll need to remove the blanket from the body and bag it for evidence first."

The two paramedics nodded.

Tye noticed that they both had on latex gloves already. *Not their first rodeo. Good sign.* "Newman can you give us a hand? Don't want to drop this poor woman tryin' to get her out."

"Sure." His face remained stoic.

"Spread out and get underneath her. She's not very heavy," Tye commented as he moved closer to the woman's head.

The other three actually had to stand shoulder to shoulder to reach into the trunk. Joel placed his hands under the victim's calves and noted that she only was wearing one shoe, a well worn cheap imitation flat.

"On three, okay?" Tye counted down and the four men easily lifted the body clear of the trunk lip. "Wheel clockwise and we can all get on one side of the gurney."

Stella watched with much emotion. She mouthed a silent prayer. *Lord, please accept your humble servant Lupe. I'm certain she believed in the resurrection, her sins are paid for through the blood of our redeemer, Jesus Christ. Amen.* A single tear ran down across her right cheek, but she made no effort to wipe it away.

A wrecker arrived to tow away the abandoned vehicle.

Stella nudged Juan. "Tell him it will be about ten minutes, okay?"

As he walked to talk to the driver, she turned away from unwrapping the victim and moved up closer to the passenger side of the Taurus. Looking inside, she spotted a small Barbie doll in the front seat. Her lower lip began to quiver and tears fell from both eyes. *Oh my God. That's about all that poor little girl has left in the world.*

She opened the door and retrieved the well-used toy.

Tye took a few pictures of the victim before the paramedics pulled up a white sheet covering her.

Stella approached Joel. "Can you handle it from here?"

He knew from experience what was going on in the head of the grieving cop. "I got it. It's way past your shift anyway."

"Thanks," she said in a low voice. Stella walked up to Juan who was still chatting with the wrecker driver. "Come on, Partner...We're outta here."

"Let's do it." He glanced down at the object clutched tightly in her hand and then locked eyes with her for a brief moment. He saw the pain clearly etched in her face. "Hey...want me to drive?"

She said nothing, but simply nodded. For most of the ride up Commerce Street to the station, she stared blankly out the patrol car window.

BONE'S RANCH
WESTERN COOKE COUNTY

"Dang, it Bone. I have to say that was probably the best hunk of fish I ever ate. Tender, moist, and just a hint of lemon with a bit of oak and mesquite smoke thrown in. How did you create that little gem?"

The huge Texan leaned back away from the table and grinned. "Remember after my stint in the

Corps, I took some time off before I went to work for the Dallas PD?"

"Yeah, you went off to Europe for a few months. Never talked about it much, as I recall. Just kinda disappeared."

"Yep…decompressed a bit after that cluster in the sand box…Well, anyway, in Paris, there are some really cool apartments overlookin' the Seine."

"Go on." Padrino leaned in closer, his attention fully on his great nephew.

"Not too far from the apartment was this well-known French cookin' school…"

"*Le Cordon Bleu*?"

"No…even more famous than that. The *École de Cuisine Alain Ducasse*. On west bank of that windy ass Seine river, 'bout a mile and a half…maybe two from the Eiffel tower. Lemme see, what was the street address? Oh, yeah…64 *Rue du Ranelagh*."

He took in a deep breath and let it out slowly. "Man, just walking past the ftont door could be an olfactory orgasmic experience in absolute culinary magic. Fresh-baked croissants."

Bone closed his eyes as a smile crossed his lips. "*Chateaubriand*, fresh herbs *de Provence*, a myriad of local cheeses, buttery escargot in olive oil and garlic, bechamel sauce…"

Bone barely opened one eye to see if Padrino was still locked in to the story. His godfather had likewise closed his eyes and was imagining the sights and smells. He was buying the story big time.. The big man roared in laughter.

Padrino opened his eyes and stared at Bone with confusion. "What's so funny?"

"The thought of me taking a formal culinary course in Paris." He chuckled. "I can't speak a lick of frog talk except for their food…you might say I'm only fluent in restaurant French."

"Damn you, Bone! You made up all that whopper?"

"Gotcha…Gotcha hook line and sinker." He grinned like a mule eating persimmons.

"You can be such a dick, sometimes. Where did you get the idea about the aluminum foil, then?"

"Our neighbor to the north…Ol' Buck told me about it when he turned me on to the Green Egg…Said he used to cook whole salmon on a gas grill when he lived in Alaska."

Bone held his hands a little over two feet apart. "Wrapped 'em in foil, and when they unwrapped it, the skin came off with it."

"I had no idea it was that easy," Padrino exclaimed.

Bone shrugged. "Buck told me he used two spatulas to lift one entire half off the rib cage…Then, he could lift out all the bones at one time and they would serve the other half…Worked like a champ at dinner parties on Elmendorf."

"I didn't know he was a vet…Air Force, I assume."

"Uh huh. Fighter pilot and transports later."

"Funny, when you see him driving a bulldozer or tractor, that pilot background doesn't come to mind." Padrino shook his head.

"You oughta see him shoot. Guy is deadly…and at long range. He was on the rifle team at the Air Force Academy."

"Never suspected that…Hell, he's almost as big as you."

"I got maybe a few inches on him. Besides. I played football. He was on the inaugural rugby team at the zoo, as he calls it."

Padrino grinned. "You know what they say about rugby, don't you?...It takes leather balls to play rugby."

Bone grinned. "I may be crazy, but I'm not that crazy. Play a contact sport with no helmets or pads." Suddenly Bone's grin faded.

"Something wrong? Padrino asked.

"Yeah...no. Not really. Thinking about Buck reminded me of a discussion we had a couple years back...Somehow, discussion turned to Tesla and energy transmissions. He told me about a demonstration he witnessed at Wright Pat Air Base back in the '60s. The Air Force was doing research on sound weapons. They could cause an aircraft's aluminum skin to fail, basically crumble, just by using a strong sonic wave."

Padrino stroked his chin. "Wouldn't that energy attenuate in the atmosphere over great distances? I can't see how such a weapon could knock down an enemy bomber or fighter from many miles away."

"You are absolutely right...It can't. That's why they never fielded an operational version. But that was only part of the demonstration...It's the other part that Stienke told me about that I just remembered." Bone sat up straight.

"Is this going to be another one of your bullcrap tall tales?"

"Not this time, amigo…See, back when he was a cadet, like fifty plus years ago, they took a group of them to a huge room with tall foam spikes on all the walls and ceilings…"

"An anechoic chamber?"

"That's the correct name, as I recall. The foam keeps sound waves from bouncing back to their source."

"So, then…what was the demonstration?"

"Buck said there were wooden planks, like two by twelves, laid end to end across the floor. They were supported off the concrete by little shorter sections of two by fours. The officers conducting the tour asked the cadets to try to walk across the room on the planks."

"What happened?"

"Well, nobody could make it across without getting dizzy or disorientated."

"That's weird. Wonder why that was?"

"Turns out the young zoomies were being targeted with very low frequency sound waves…Well below the threshold of human hearing…Fifteen to twenty hertz."

"You mean like cycles per second? That's very low. What could it possibly do to a human body to disrupt it if you can't hear it?"

"That's the thing…ever hear of something called resonant frequency?"

"As in the frequency at which an object begins to vibrate?"

Bone nodded. "Precisely. At an object's resonant frequency small input forces have the ability to produce large amplitude oscillations, due to the storage of vibrational energy. Later research seems to indicate the human body has a resonant frequency of five hertz. The head and heart, when isolated…are slightly higher."

"What does all this have to do with anything?"

Bone took in a deep breath. He held up both hands to make a point. "Okay, here's the straight skinny. A low amplitude fifteen hertz wave could make young Cadet Stienke's heart bounce around inside his chest. He felt strange…like something was about to bust inside him and he fell off the wooden plank."

Bone paused and focused his vision on Padrino. "What would have happened if they used a high amplitude invisible, inaudible sound wave?"

Padrino's eyes grew wide. "Oh my God…I didn't connect the dots. Can resonant frequency vibrations rip apart a heart?"

"From what I saw at Doc Fisk's office, I have to say the answer is most definitely…yes."

"That sounds like some sort of death ray."

A random thought struck Bone like a bolt of lightning. "Doctor Hans Zarkov! Brilliant scientist who created a death ray."

"When did that happen? I never heard of him."

"Then you must not ever have read the Buck Rogers comic books."

Padrino raised his eyebrows. "Buck Rogers? Not my taste. I preferred the Blackhawks and Captain America. Was that Doctor Zarkov an evil mastermind bent to take over the world?"

"Nah, that would be what you call the Zarkov Paradox. He was brilliant and he created a death ray to save the Earth from the truly evil Ming the Merciless, tyrant from the planet Mongo."

Padrino smiled. "I'm so glad you cleared that up… All you have to do now is find the modern descendant of a fictional character who found his ancestor's death ray gun in the attic." He chuckled to himself.

"Don't ever try your hand at standup. The world is not ready for you."

Bone pushed back from the table and reached for a bottle of Patron on the top shelf in the kitchen. He grabbed a crystal highball glass and filled it halfway with ice from the fridge. Popping the top off the silver label tequila, he poured three fingers into the glass and then pounded the stopper home.

"I see you have some cogitatin' to do. You cooked the fish, so I'll clean up...Good luck, Detective." Padrino began to pick up the plates.

Bone sauntered slowly to his recliner and set down easily, so not to spill the nectar of the agave.

He took a sip and savored the flavor of his go-to choice of hard liquor. His eyes scanned the walls until they found a picture of his old Marine Corps unit in Afghanistan. The younger men were all decked out in full desert camo battle rattle. Their faces were covered in dirt layered on top of green and black camo paint. His eyes focused on a major standing to his left. He sat the glass down and pulled out a tattered address book from the wooden lamp stand set between the recliners.

§§§

CHAPTER EIGHT

GAINESVILLE POLICE STATION

Juan dropped the keys to the cruiser with the desk sergeant. Stella had become a little more composed by the time they had reached the station. He looked at her before he turned to leave the building. "Hey partner, would you like to grab a beer or something? Been a rough day."

"That is has. Maybe some other time. I got a couple calls to make. Still have to set up a BOLO on Miguel Santiago."

"Oh yeah. Forgot about that little detail."

She shrugged. "It doesn't get done if we don't do it. The investigators are more into laying out the court case at this point."

"Need some help?"

She waved him off. "I'm okay now. Well almost. Get outta here, tomorrow's another day."

"See ya." He turned and headed to door.

Stella addressed the duty sergeant, Terry Anderson—a chubby forty year old who was looking forward to retiring in another two years. "Hey, Sarge, do I need to contact the Captain to issue a BOLO for a murder suspect?"

"No, pretty lady. I can do that in his absence. Who are we looking out for?"

She pulled out the picture that she had folded up in her purse. "Miguel Santiago, Hispanic male, age early twenties. Five feet seven, weight about one hundred fifty, brown hair and eyes. Last seen on a southbound Santa Fe passenger train. Suspect wanted in the murder of his wife, Lupe Santiago."

His hands were flying on his desktop keyboard. "Any known aliases? How about an address?"

Stella handed him the printout from St. Mary's. "No known alias. He was driving a Ford Taurus, but left it with his wife's body inside, at the depot."

"That's the one Newman called in. I sent Tye to cover it. You say he's on a train?"

"Got the schedule right here...Too late for Temple, but they can intercept him in Round Rock if they move fast." She the handed him the printout from the ticket master.

Terry checked his wrist watch. "That's doable. I'll ring up the Rangers and the Round Rock PD. You did a hell of a job, Stella."

"Thanks. It kinda all fell together...for a change."

"Go home...You look beat."

"Not yet. Not till they see if Santiago is still on the train."

"Your call, young lady...Lauri made some fresh coffee for the evening shift before she boogied."

Stella nodded. "Think I will. Don't imagine I could sleep tonight anyway."

BONE'S PARADOX

BONE'S RANCH
WESTERN COOKE COUNTY

Bone came across a name from the past in his well-worn address book. He took another sip of the tequila and reached for his cell phone.

Tyrin climbed up in his lap. "Settle down you big lug. I know you missed me. I can't stay home all day and play with you." He rubbed behind the pit bull's ears. "If you behave, you can stay while I make my call." Tyrin seemed to smile.

Bone tapped in the Dallas number and added it to his contact list. He hit the call button and it rang.

In an upscale home in North Dallas, a lantern-jawed forty-nine year old man was seated at his desk in a lavishly furnished man cave. The walls were adorned with pictures of himself, and various units, along with photo of him with Presidents and Senators. He reached for his cell phone when it rang and glanced at the caller ID. He didn't recognize the incoming number.

"Hello, this is Don speaking."

"Major Martine?"

"It's Colonel Martine, these days."

"Sorry...Congraulations on the promotions, sir. This is Darrell Bone...I served under you in the Corps...Afghanistan...Captain in Force Recon."

A flicker of recognition crossed his face then it bloomed into a full-fledged smile. "Bone! How the hell are you, you big galloot? Ooorah! Semper Fi!...Last I heard, you were with the Dallas PD."

"Semper Fi...Been a detective up here with the Gainesville PD for a few years...Long story. Won't bore you with the mundane. Maybe over a few beers sometime."

"What's going on?"

"Well, Colonel, I've got a multiple homicide case that's kickin' my butt in a major fashion. Wonder if you could shed some light on it?"

"Don't know if I can be of any help or not...What are some of the details?"

"The vics...sorry, I slipped right into my cop talk...The victims suffered from massive traumatic internal injuries. Two had brains that looked like they'd been imploded and the third, a woman had her heart ripped apart in four or five places."

"Bone, you know there are a lot of ways to cause injuries that you describe."

"But not in a couple seconds, with zero sound, and no external marks…not even so much as a bruise. "

Colonel Martine's face clouded up. He set the phone down flat and tapped the icon for the speaker phone. "You are saying they were murdered in a matter of seconds?"

"According to witnesses in the first case, the guy was fine one minute and stone cold dead seconds later, with blood coming out his nose and eyes. Almost like a death ray zapped him."

"Mother of God." The Marine officer's brow furrowed deeply. "That's rather disturbing."

"Kinda my thought on the subject…I've been keeping up with some of the area denial weapons the US Army and Marine Corps were developing back in my day. Any of those ever make to the field? "

"Sure, the Army has the Active Denial System…basically a huge microwave transmitter mounted on a Humvee and a big truck mounted generator. We use them at some of our embassies overseas where lethal force is too politically sensitive."

"I'm familiar with that. They use ninety-five gigahertz beams to heat up the top layer of the skin. And you are correct…they are friggin' huge. What about lasers?"

"My friend, we have lasers that can take down aircraft and missiles…but the heat generated to burn though metal would vaporize skin and bone…no pun intended."

"Gotcha. That's the conclusion I came to as well. Sherlock Holmes once said, "Eliminate the obvious and whatever you have left, however improbable, is the truth."

"And what would that be?"

"My gut tells me that someone invented a low frequency sonic weapon. You know, down in the ten to twenty Hertz range? Something small, man portable…Operating just below the threshold of human hearing, it resonates the human body until their insides rupture. No visible laser light, no sound…just death from afar on demand." Bone petted Tyrin's neck. "As I recall, you did a stint at DARPA after we left Kabul."

The colonel swallowed at the lump that was beginning to develop in his throat. "Still associated with them."

Bone took a sip of Patron. "Guess I'll just have to cut to the chase, sir. Are you guys working on a lethal ray weapon that can cause these types of mortal wounds that I've described?"

"If someone developed such a portable low frequency sonic weapon, they would have found the Holy Grail of weapon technology."

Bone's dark eyes narrowed. "You didn't answer my question, Colonel. Are you guys working on a sonic weapon?

Colonel Martine frowned. "Bone, your Top Secret Security Clearance expired five years after you left the Corps. Under the security laws of the United States, I can neither confirm nor deny that such a weapon exists."

Bone smiled. "You just did...I know when and where. All I have to figure out is who and why."

"Listen my friend, if someone came up with a fully operational model like you describe and is off the reservation, so to speak...I can't tell you how dangerous they could be. Do not try to take them down solo. You hear what I'm saying?"

"I'm listening."

"Call me if you get a lead. I can pull some strings with a two star in Special Ops. He owes me big time."

"Appreciate the offer, Colonel, but I don't have a clue as the who the suspect would be at this point. The arrival of some black helicopter federal task force might just send the purp underground…Great talking to you. I'll keep in touch."

"Same here," Martine said as he took note of Bone's phone number.

"Laterbye." Bone ended the call and flipped his cell cover closed. He drained the crystal glass. And set it back on the lamp table. He stroked Tryin's neck and the dog rolled over on its back. "You are gettin's spoiled rotten, you know that?"

Tyrin's hind legs beat a tattoo as Bone rubbed his belly and grinned.

AMTRAK RAILROAD DEPOT
AUSTIN

Captain Joseph Robert Anderson, Texas Ranger commander of the detachment in Austin checked his watch. *7:47 They're running a few minutes late.*

He glanced to his right. A single uniformed cop was stationed on the street side of the depot. Four other Austin cops in tactical gear and three additional Rangers were out of sight, awaiting Anderson's order to move in.

The late summer sun was setting when the Texas Eagle pulled into the station. Eleven people disembarked. None of them matched the physical description of Miguel Santiago.

Joseph, known as Joe Bob to his team, wore an earpiece with tiny boom mike in his left ear. His starched white western shirt covered level III soft body armor. A white straw Stetson sat atop his head, partially covering his closely cropped crew cut. "Move in," he directed on their team's tactical frequency.

Anderson stepped forward to the front of the first of four passenger cars. As briefed, the other Rangers took the similar entrances on the other three cars with the Austin SWAT team members taking a blocking position at the rear of each car.

The Ranger captain rapidly scanned each face in the sparsely crowded rail car. Only one matched the picture sent from the Gainesville PD. "Suspect in car one. Two rows from the back. Positive ID," he said in a low voice.

His right hand dropped to the grip of his custom Colt Gold Cup 1911. His thumb opened the retention strap on his holster as his fingers wrapped tightly around the stag handles. "Texas Ranger! Stay in your seats!" he called out as the burly APD SWAT officer took up a blocking position at the far end of the rail car. He locked eyes with the suddenly apprehensive fugitive. "Miguel Santiago. *Estas bajo arresto...levanta las manos*!"

Miguel jumped up and pivoted toward the back door. He caught himself and lurched backward at the sight of the six foot three inch cop in full tactical gear filling the doorway. The .45 muzzle on the officer's Sig 220 looked as big as a storm drain to the citizen of Mexico. He spun around and faced the gringo in the cowboy hat that had closed the distance between them considerably.

None of the other passengers got a great look at what happened next. Most had ducked low in their seats and were trying to stay out of harm's way.

The teenager returning home to San Antonio had been seated across the aisle from Miguel. He curled back against the far wall when he saw the flash of razor sharp silver as the Hispanic man pushed the button on the switchblade he held in his right hand.

"Knife!" Joe Bob shouted as he drew the highly polished stainless Colt out of its holster. He brought it up almost to eye level and yelled "drop it" as the young illegal alien leaned forward and charged him.

Miguel screamed, "*Pendejo!*"

Three shots rang out almost as one. Inside the closed car, the thunderous sound was painfully loud.

Two rounds struck the suspect three inches below his Adam's apple. The third made a dime-sized hole in the top on his skull as he fell forward. The killer's body landed on the passenger car floor with a dull thud. The switchblade clattered across the carpet and came to rest inches from the Ranger's pointed boot.

GAINESVILLE POLICE DEPARTMENT

Stella was staring blankly at the computer screen in the common area when her cell phone broke her trance. It took her a second to find it in her handbag. She glanced at the caller ID. *Somebody from the Austin area code.*

"Hello, this is Stella."

"Officer Johnson, I'm Captain Anderson, of the Texas Rangers."

"Yes, sir. How may I help you?"

"I don't need any help, Ma'am. I just wanted to let you know that we intercepted the fugitive Miguel Santiago down in Austin."

"Did you catch him?

"No, Ma'am. Not exactly. He didn't let us take him alive...Boy brought a knife to gun fight and Mister Santiago died of his wounds. Your sergeant filled me in on the case, and I thought that you earned the right to hear how it went down."

Stella took in a deep breath. "Thank you, Captain. That very nice of you."

"No, Officer Johnson, thank you. We wouldn't have got him in time if you hadn't made the case for us. Say...if you're ever down in River City, look me up. Be rather proud to buy you a beer."

She smiled a little. "Might just do that. Thanks again. Good night."

Stella hit the tiny icon and ended the call. She looked at the partially completed supplemental report on her computer. She saved the work and signed out. *It will still be here in the morning.*

BONE'S PARADOX

She stared at the tiny little Barbie doll looking a bit forlorn on the table. Her eyes rimmed with tears as she picked it up. *They got him. He didn't get away with what he did.*

§§§

CHAPTER NINE

GAINESVILLE POLICE STATION

Loraine walked into the office at 0635, almost an hour and a half earlier than usual. The sight of Bone seated at this desk stopped her in her tracks. "What are you doin here? Do you know what time it is?"

"I work here…remember?" He rubbed both eyes with his fingertips. "Been up since three-thirty.

Couldn't sleep." He yawned and covered his gaping mouth with the back of his right hand. "Sorry...What time is it, anyway?"

"Half past six...Couldn't sleep either. You need some coffee, big boy?"

"You bet, I made a full pot about five or so. Should be a few cups left."

Loraine set her purse down on her desk. She picked up his empty mug. "Be right back in a flash." She walked out the door and headed for the break room. As she stepped inside, she spotted forensic technician Peach Presley pouring the coffee down the sink.

The tall brunette had a frown on her face and she shook her head as she spoke in a deep Georgia accent. "I'll swannie, some folks round here act just like they were raised in a barn...All proper and decent people know to pour out this old nasty java at the end of the day shift."

"Except Bone just made it fresh 'bout five this morning."

Peach turned around and blushed. "Oh, well hush my mouth, Loraine...didn't know anybody else was here in the office yet. I'll make us some more in a jiffy."

"Bone and I would appreciate it…Kinda early start for us."

"Uh huh." Peach measured the ground coffee and poured it into the gold plated permanent filter. "This string of murders has got me more than a little puckered up. Been running the lab tests twice to make sure I get the same results." She filled the glass coffee pot with water and then poured it into the coffee maker and hit the brew button.

"Anything out of the ordinary on the toxicology?"

Peach shook her head and pouted ever so slightly. "Butter my butt and call me a biscuit. For the life of me, cannot find any sign of poison…Just a minor trace of THC in the vic pulled from the pool."

"Okay, so our male model DB smoked a little weed recently…don't think that has any tie-in with the cause of death."

The attractive tall technician shrugged. "Not likely." She turned around to check on the status of the brew. "A couple more minutes, sugar. So sorry I messed up the pot Bone made."

Loraine laughed. "Another minute wait will not kill that big galoot."

Peach laughed. "It would take a heap more than a little caffeine shortage to lay that leviathan low."

The coffee maker finished it's cycle.

Loraine retrieved her personal mug off the break room peg board. She held out hers and Bone's for Miss Presley. "Fill 'em up with Ethyl. Bone and I have got a lot of work ahead of us."

Peach complied. "We all do. I'll try to get y'all a printout of my lab work up through this point before eight o'clock."

"Appreciate it. Will let the big man know."

Bone tilted his mug back and drained the last of the hot black brew. "That's seriously nasty joe...I really need to buy the department some decent grind."

"I second that," Loraine said as she took a sip. The bitterness of the bargain basement brew made her shiver a tiny bit.

"What doesn't kill you makes you stronger...except for bears. Bears will just friggin' kill you." Bone set his mug down and raised both hands up with his fingers curled slightly, pantomiming a bear attack.

Loraine chuckled. "Sure you don't have Shiner Bock in there instead of coffee?"

He grinned. "Anyway, as I was sayin', Colonel Martine more or less confirmed that the United States military has been working on some sonic weapons. I already knew that from a discussion I had with my neighbor."

"He couldn't be specific?"

"Not on an unsecured line. This stuff is Top Secret…Maybe higher than Top Secret, say NOFORN."

Loraine nodded.

Bone scratched his head. "When I got here this mornin', I Googled sonic weapons. Most of it was the usual BS about the Army's area denial weapons…you know the ADS that can make you feel like your skin's on fire?"

Loraine shook her head with something of a deer in the headlights look. "Pretend I know nothing about that military stuff…"

Bone shook his head. "Only 'cause you really don't know nothing 'bout this kind of thing. I forget…Anyway I find a little link to a treasure trove of info on the French, Germans, Ruskies, Chinese, Brits…You know…basically all our NATO allies and major geopolitical adversaries."

"Wait...what does that have to do with these cases?" Loraine had a puzzled look on her face.

"Permit me to finish, oh ye of very little worldly travels...As I was going to say, they all have been developing sonic weapons in secret."

"That's peachy keeno. So our list of suspects just went from local to global."

"Possibly." Bone thought for second. "Not sure if the good colonel was holding out on me or what...but I learned a lot about resonance and infrasound and what frequencies affect what body parts and functions in my last three hours on the web."

"Infrasound?"

"Pay attention, girl." Bone grinned. "Class is now in session...Infrasound is the range known as ELF or extremely low frequency...way down there between one and twenty hertz."

"Like the rental car company?"

"No, knothead...Spelled the same, but is equivalent to a cycle per second."

"And that's below the human threshold of hearing?"

"Uh huh…As it turns out, the ELF frequencies can cause resonance in human body and probably cause the injuries we saw over at Doc Fisk's."

Loraine's face furrowed. "So a bad person can use a sonic weapon that could injure or kill without breaking the skin?"

"You catch on fast…A new kind of silent, but deadly." He grinned.

She ignored his attempt at humor. "Wow that's kinda scary. Almost like something from Buck Rogers or Flash Gordon…"

"Except they don't use a laser. This thing didn't burn the skin.…Actually, I don't know how the hell it works or even what it could look like…Just know it works. We saw proof of that over in the morgue."

Loraine nodded in agreement. "Like Doctor Zarkov's Death Ray from Flash Gordon." She crossed her arms as she pondered the predicament. "If we don't know who did it, maybe we should focus on why."

Bone sat silent for a moment, looking almost like he was in a trance. He jumped to his feet. "Damn, Pard! That's it! You're a freaking genius." He donned his hat, leaned over and kissed her on the forehead.

"What's it? Suddenly I'm a genius? You been drinkin' again?"

"Only three fingers of Patron." He held up one hand. "Honest Injun...Come on, Pard, Grab your gear."

"Where are we off to in such a rush?"

"To the courthouse, silly...Gotta find the why."

Loraine crossed her arms and gave him a look. "Cool your jets, sky pilot. There's nobody there for another hour and fifteen minutes."

Bone checked his watch. His enthusiasm waned considerably. "Oh." He took off his hat and hung it on the rack. "Sometimes I hate it when you're right." He sank into his chair and made a sad face—merely for theatrical purposes.

Loraine smiled and opened up her laptop.

§§§

CHAPTER TEN

COOKE COUNTY COURTHOUSE

Bone and Loraine took the stairs up the third floor of the mostly deserted building. They made their way down the marbled halls to a series of offices.

"This looks like the right one," Bone said as he checked out the name tag engraved in black plastic beside the entrance. He held the door open for his partner. Loraine entered and Bone followed close behind her.

Inside the walnut paneled office was a small outer room where the judge's assistant had her desk. There was no one there. Loraine looked at her partner and shrugged.

Bone pointed at the closed door to the judge's private office and grinned. He approached the door, knocked once and opened it. The scent of an expensive French perfume drifted past Bone. A beautiful blonde woman was filling heavy boxes on the mahogany desk with books, plagues and photos. She looked up at the unexpected visitors and her face conveyed a slightly startled look.

"Hi, I'm Detective Bone with the Gainesville PD." He motioned towards the much smaller woman. "This is my partner, Inspector Loraine Rodriguez." He extended his hand.

The woman locked eyes with him and then Loraine. She extended her hand to greet Bone. "I'm Cindy Tanner...I am...I was...Judge Lockhart's administrative assistant." Her voice cracked as she spoke.

Bone took her hand. Visions of a sunny secluded beach and a nude middle aged man and an attractive younger woman—also au natural—flooded his consciousness. Those images were quickly replaced with the same naked man in a large brass bed with many frilly pillows propping him up—only to be swept away by a scene of the same man lying on the sidewalk outside, bloodied and still.

Bone felt an almost electric shock as he released her delicate hand. "I'm so sorry for your loss. I imagine that you two were…very close."

Cindy wiped back a tear. "Yes, we worked together for years, four days a week."

Bone nodded. *I bet you did. Wonder how many nights you burned the midnight oil as well?* He glanced at a framed photograph one of the boxes. The judge was in his robe an standing beside the US flag. "Never had the pleasure to meet the gentleman." He turned and spotted a larger picture of the judge, a woman and two children. "I take it he was married?"

"That's a picture of his wife Dorothy, and son Skip and daughter Pat. Both of the kids are attending Texas A&M University." She gazed up at Bone's hat and then all the way down to his custom ostrich skin boots. "I'm sorry...it's just that I don't think I've ever seen a policeman as big as you."

"They grow them big on his planet," Loraine said without cracking a smile.

Bone gave her a look and arched a single eyebrow.

Cindy gathered herself a bit. "Is there something I can help you with?"

Bone nodded. "You bet. Just a couple questions...Know anyone who would want to harm Judge Lockhart?"

"Heavens no," she said as she shook her head vigorously. "The Judge was well respected by every person who worked with him...I thought that he died of natural causes."

Bone shrugged. "We're not sure of that. The autopsy was ...uh, inconclusive. What type of cases did he handle?"

"Civil matters, divorces, child support, probate and so forth. It's not like he was dealing with murderers and real criminals." She furrowed her brow slightly.

"Uh huh...would it be possible to get a printout of all his cases over the last two years? Just the names of the parties involved, their attorneys and the type of cases for starters." He glanced at Loraine. "Anything else we need, Pard?"

"No, think that about covers the bases."

Cindy smiled weakly. "Sure thing…Should be no problem. I have his schedule in my computer. I'll have it compiled before lunch."

Bone gave her one of his patented grins. "Thanks, Cindy, you're a doll…See you in a couple of hours."

Bone and Loraine made their way out of the judge's chambers and started down the wide marble staircase.

Loraine elbowed him. "What do you think, big boy?"

He shook his head and held a finger up to his lips. When they reached the landing between floors he motioned for her to move closer. "These dang marble floors are like an echo chamber. The walls have ears."

"What?"

He turned his right palm flat and made an up and down motion. "Keep your voice down. It carries like a megaphone in this old building."

"Oh. Sorry…got it," she whispered.

Bone smiled broadly. "Had an...uh, let's say...interesting psychic connection with the comely Miss Tanner when we met."

Loraine's eyes grew wide. "Really? You mean like with you and Lucy?"

He nodded. "Yeppers...Only this time it was X rated," he chuckled.

"What? What are you talking about?"

"I saw the dearly departed barrister and his erstwhile administrator nude on a beach and him naked in what has to be her bedroom. Then I saw him sprawled out on the sidewalk in full color, three D."

"Get out! You mean..."

"Yessum, little blonde bombshell legal assistant Cindy was bopping the boss on the side."

"Another office romance goes down in flames...I wonder if his wife knew?"

"Good question, Pard. I might have you do the intro when we question the widow Dorothy. You might need to practice your empathic skills a bit in the meantime."

"I'll work on it. What's next? Wanna go back to the office?

"Nah. Got a loose end I need to tie up here first."

Loraine looked perplexed. "And that would be?"

"Brittany Wilson…want to find out how she came to own that horse ranch. It takes some serious geetus to buy a spread like that, and I'm kinda curious to find out where it came from."

GAINESVILLE POLICE STATION

Stella and Juan pulled up in front of the building and parked in the public parking area. She glanced over at her young partner. "I won't be but a minute…Wanna stay here and hold down the fort?

He shook his head. "No Ma'am. 'Bout time for a a little pause for the cause…That coffee has done all the good it can and now it's time to say good bye."

She shut off the ignition and pulled out the key. "Meet you back here in…What…three minutes? That enough time?"

"Oh sure. I'll be Speedy Gonzales."

Stella grinned for the first time that day. "Thought you told me your last name was Gomez."

"And you said all us rookies look alike."

Entering the building, Stella walked quickly toward her personal equipment locker . She waved at the dispatcher. "Hey, Lauri."

"Hey, girl friend. What's up?"

Stella waved her hand. "Nothing much…Just needed to retrieve something from my locker." She passed the break area and went directly to the women's locker room. She spun the combination on the brass padlock, twisted it free and opened the battleship gray steel door. Inside, were a spare set of patrol uniforms, extra pantyhose and an assortment of personal and toiletry items. Taped to the door were pictures of her brothers and parents.

Lying silently on the small top shelf was a well-worn Barbie doll. With almost a slight sense of trepidation she reached up and took hold of the toy. As she stared at the smudged doll face, her eyes rimmed with tears. *Lord Jesus, give me the strength to help little Carmen face the tragedy of losing both parents at so young an age.*

She closed her locker door and fastened the lock.

Juan exited the men's room and joined Stella as she walked toward the front door. He spotted the doll in her left hand. "Lemme guess…Next stop CPS."

"You don't mind, do you? It's the very least we can do." There was a deep sadness in her voice.

§

CHAPTER ELEVEN

COOKE COUNTY COURTHOUSE

Bone and Loraine walked into the County Clerk's Office. He walked up the long wooden counter and smiled at the middle-aged woman seated behind a nearby desk as he unclipped the detective badge from his Texas Ranger style belt.

Buck Stienke

"Mornin', Ma'am. Wonderin' if we could ask you a few questions."

The clerk got to her feet and bellied up to the counter. Her name tag said *Abigail Pritzer.* She warmed up as she addressed her first customers of the day. "Surely. What I can I do for you folks?"

Bone laid his badge on the counter. "Gainesville PD, Miss Pritzer…We would like some information about any properties out on One Horse Lane owned by a Miss Brittany Wilson."

The woman smiled, put on her reader glasses and studied the badge for a few seconds. "Everybody calls me Abbie." She reached under the counter and dragged out a heavy leather-bound ledger book and laid it on the counter top. The thick binder was marked *W-X.*

"We'll have that info you need in two shakes of a lambs tail." She gazed up at Bone towering over her. "You know, I don't think I've ever met a policeman as big as you."

Loraine and Bone exchanged glances. He shook his head almost imperceptibly.

Loraine ignored the signal completely. "Yes, you know the old saying…Too big for football and the circus is not hiring these days."

124

Abigail and Loraine shared a laugh.

Bone let out a small sigh and gave his partner a slightly disgusted look.

Abbie flipped through a few of the large legal sized pages. She turned over a couple more and nodded to herself. "Uh huh. Here's the one you want... Brittany Michelle Wilson was registered as the sole owner of record on that piece of property just two months ago. No lien is shown." She spun the ledger around so that Bone and Loraine could read it.

Bone scanned it quickly. "She bought it outright? From whom?"

Abbie shook her head. "I'm sorry, sir...you misunderstood. I didn't say she bought it...It was part of her divorce decree. The file makes reference to an action entitled Brittany Wilson Knight vs Philip Kent Knight, proceeding for divorce." She flipped back a page and pointed to the printing in the center of the page.

Bone's jaw fell slack as he and Loraine stared at each other. "I'll be a suck egg mule," he muttered. "Any chance that the presiding judge was named Lockhart?"

Abbie's brow furrowed as her affable smile melted into a frown. She pointed to the signature at the bottom of the page. "Why, yes it was…Isn't that just terrible what happened to Judge Lockhart? Everybody loved him."

Bone slipped his cell phone out of his pocket and opened the cover. He took a picture of the page and then flipped it back to the previous one and recorded a picture of it as well. "Almost everybody…Thanks, Abbie, you're an angel." He tipped his hat to the clerk and closed the cover on his cell.

Bone knocked once as he opened the door to Judge Lockhart's office. Cindy Tanner was seated at her desk and typing on the keyboard. She looked up, a bit surprised at the duo's quick return.

"I'm sorry, Detective, but I'm not quite finished with the report you asked for."

"That's okay, Miss." He opened his cell phone and expanded the picture of the settlement decree. "Just need the Knight vs Knight distribution of properties from this past April."

"Cindy's eyes grew wider. "Oh, I remember that one. Lot's of money in that settlement…She did quite well as I recall."

Loraine nodded. "Maybe too well…She's dead now."

Cindy gasped and covered her mouth. "I'm so sorry. Didn't know…"

Bone cut her off. "Reminds me of an old Jerry Reed song…'She got the gold mine and he got the shaft'…We'd like to get a copy of the full settlement on that one and the names of all the attorneys involved."

"Okay, I'll have that in a second or two." Cindy nodded and her fingers flew across the key board. A few moves with a mouse later, she left clicked it and then hit the *print* icon. The high speed printer beside her desk began to rapidly spit out several sheets of legal sized paper.

"You don't think the attorneys did anything wrong, do you?" Cindy's face mirrored her concern.

Loraine shook her head. "No…but they may be in danger."

Cindy turned and grabbed the short stack, tapped it on her desk to align the edges, and then stapled them neatly in the upper left corner.

Bone glanced at the papers and scanned quickly through the top four pages. "Thank you ever so much, Cindy girl...Tell you what...hold off on the rest of his schedule unless I call you back...Have a gut feeling this is all that we're gonna need."

She smiled sweetly and said, "You can call me anytime." She wrinkled her nose slightly and winked.

"You never know, darlin'. Might just do that." Bone tipped his hat. "Come on, Pard. Got what we came for...we're burning' daylight."

"Right." She tilted her head toward Cindy. "Appreciate your help, Miss Tanner." She followed Bone out the door and closed it behind her. Several yards away from the office, she glared up at Bone.

"I can't believe how she threw herself at you. How brazen was that?" Loraine whispered and subsequently pursed her lips.

Bone broke out into a huge grin. "What? You call that flirtin'? Hah...She didn't even take off an item of intimate apparel for a remembrance..."

"Men!" she hissed. "You think every woman you meet wants to jump your bones...no pun intended." She backhanded him across the chest.

"Watch it, hot rod, you coulda broken my favorite pocket mirror."

"And besides, she probably wasn't wearing any panties...I know her type," she hissed.

Bone chuckled. They reached the stairwell and started down. He glanced over at her. "You know, now that you mention it...I didn't see a panty line under that tight little skirt she was wearin'. Maybe you're on to somethin'."

"Oh my God...I put your libido into turbo boost."

Bone laughed. "Why is it that you are suddenly getting all jealous? Have you fallen under my spell as well?" He winked.

"In your wildest, wettest dreams, you...you overgrown penis with legs." Her face began to turn bright red.

"Don't fight it, woman. It's Kismet...Written in the stars." He winked his other eye.

"Grrr. I think I'm gonna blow chunks."

"You look ravishing when you're confused and in the presence of dominant male pheromones. I've seen it happen before...Many times"

GAINESVILLE CPS OFFICES

Stella pulled into the parking spot marked *OFFICIAL USE ONLY* and put the patrol unit into park. She turned to Juan. "You don't have to go in if you don't want to, you know."

"Hey, dummy. You don't hardly speak a lick of Spanish. What are you planning to tell her?"

"Oh, my gosh…I'm not sure. Really want her to have her Barbi doll. She needs to know her mother is not coming for her."

"You not gonna tell her that her father killed her mom, are you?" Juan had a look of concern.

Stella shook her head rapidly. "Way too early to tell her that…Might traumatize a three year old."

"I would think. We do need to tell her that her aunt will be her new guardian."

"I know…I read somewhere that the best way to give some tragic news is to break it slowly."

Juan nodded. "Yeah…Think that would help Carmen digest it bit by bit."

Stella reached up and turned off the unit. "This is one of the worst parts of the whole Protect and Serve gig…You know?"

"Without a doubt. But we'll do it as a team, okay?"

Stella forced a smile. "Okay."

Inside the single story building, the pair found the receptionist's simple gray steel desk. Several stackable fiberglass chairs were lining the walls in the sparsely furnished office. An older, fairly heavyset black woman was working behind the desk. Her desk name tag said Latoya Washington. Stella spoke first, "Good morning. We're here to see Carmen Santiago."

"Y'all got an appointment?" Latoya replied.

"No...nothing like that. I found a toy that belonged to her and wanted to see that she gets it." Stella held up the doll.

Latoya held out her hand. "Ya'll can leave it with me...I sees that she gets it."

Juan glanced at Stella. "We really need to talk to her. Carmen's parents are both recently deceased and her aunt on her mother's side will be coming up from Fort Worth to take custody."

Latoya frowned. "I don't know nothin' 'bout all that. Nobody gets to see any of our clients without approval from my manager." She crossed her arms.

131

Stella placed both of her hands on the desk. "In that case, we'd like to see your manager."

Latoya smiled, exposing a wide gap between her two front teeth. "She be gone to lunch and be back 'round one thirty or two."

Juan looked at his watch. "It's only nine thirty now."

Latoya nodded. "Guess she be really hongry."

Stella stared at the uncooperative woman. "Can you at least tell me where Carmen is?"

Ms. Washington shook her head slowly. "Not without permission from my manager."

Stella glanced at Juan. She could tell he was getting fed up with the run-around as well. She tilted her head toward the door. "Let's go. There's someone I need to talk to."

Juan nodded and then looked Latoya in the eye. "We'll be back...you can count on that."

Outside, he quizzed Stella. "What kind of bullshit was that?"

"Don't know, but next stop is City Hall. I'm gonna have a few choice words with the City Manager and see if we can light a fire under CPS."

"I'm with ya."

BONE'S PARADOX

They climbed in the black and gold painted patrol unit. Stella set the Barbie on the center console.

§

CHAPTER TWELVE

GAINESVILLE POLICE DEPARTMENT

Bone and Loraine were both seated at their respective desks, wearing out their laptop keyboards.

He pushed back from the desk and exhaled loudly. "Damn."

She looked across the aisle. "Any luck tracking his present location?"

"Zippo. No utilities, cell phones or property listings in any of the north Texas counties for a Philip K. Knight. It's like the guy did a complete Houdini after his divorce...Finding anything?"

"The DuckDuckGo web search results are fascinating...Really incredible. The guy's in the Who's Who In America in Science. BS from Cal Tech...Ph.D. in Physics from MIT. Real whiz kid. Holds multiple patents in quantum physics, computer design and nanotechnology."

Bone leaned forward and propped his left elbow on the desk—resting his jaw in his hand as he processed her findings. "Jeez, that's just the kind of brain it would take to create a sonic weapon." He hit *Enter* on a search of NCIC, a nationwide criminal database.

His eyes narrowed as the report was generated. "Dammit. Nothing on a criminal record...Just a couple speeding tickets...maybe ten years ago. He's never been handled, but the boy is still at the top of my list."

Loraine's face lit up. "Whoa, Nellie. Wait a minute, Mister Bennett...Here's a pic from a *D* magazine layout on him. Who does that look like to you?"

It was a color picture of an attractive young couple lounging at a pool.

Bone ambled to his feet and leaned over her shoulder. "Don't know, but I'd sure like her number. She's smokin' hot...sweet."

Loraine glared up at her partner. "Not her, dummy...Him."

Bone leaned in closer and studied the smiling man's picture. His face slowly reflected recognition and then quickly turned to anger. "Sumbitch! That's the friggin' pool guy...without the goatee and longer hair. That murderin' bastard was right in our hands...He's playing us!"

Loraine turned and eyeballed Bone. "Not any more."

Bone returned to his office chair and sat down. "Just thought of somethin'." He closed his eyes and brought his huge palms close together—with all ten fingertips touching.

Loraine watched curiously as his eyeballs moved under his closed lids and his head twitched slightly.

After a few minutes, he opened his eyes. "That cheeky bastard."

"What are you babbling about?"

Bone pointed a finger at her. "Remember when we drove up to the Wilson Estate on One Horse Lane?"

She nodded. "Of course."

"I suppose you recall the GPD unit parked in front of the house?"

"Sure…Joel Newman's unit. What about it?"

Bone shook his head. "Not that vehicle…The white Ford panel truck with *Philip's Pool Service* painted on the sides and back."

She shrugged. "Don't remember…Where was it?"

"About ninety yards off the paved entrance drive, out by the row of shrubs lining the back yard."

"But how…"

He folded his arms. "Remember that mental concentration trick that Lucy taught us? The time we had to learn all those spacecraft systems on the short-short?"

"You mean to say…"

"Look at nothing…see everything." He grinned. "Our minds are like a high def cell phone camera.

They pick it tiny little details…all the time. We just have to learn to focus to remember them."

"Can you recall the truck license plate number?" Loraine was incredulous.

"Is a bullfrog waterproof?"

She made a face. "You're full of it like a Christmas goose."

Bone feigned his pride was hurt. "Oh, ye heathen who's faith is to be found lacking." He closed his eyes once more. A few seconds later, he opened them. "All right, resident skeptic…Run this plate: BRF-162…Texas of course."

"Of course." Loraine opened a new window and accessed the *Law Enforcement Only* section of the Texas Department of Motor Vehicles website. A few clicks later, she entered the tag number. The results irritated her. "Dammit to hell…That can't possibly right."

"Whatcha got, my little doubting Thomas?"

"It says the plate is registered to a brand new Cadillac Escalade, owned by none other than Brittany Wilson."

Bone grinned. He cupped one hand behind his left ear. "Hear that?"

"Hear what?"

"Violin music…Don't you hear it?"

Loraine face mirrored her perplexed condition. She turned her head one way and then the other, listening intently. She shrugged.

Bone grinned. "I still hear it. Sounds like a Stradivarius to me…Old Phil is still playin' us…At least one of us." He raised one eyebrow.

"Bastard." She grabbed a Bic ball point pen off her desk and flung it at him.

He snatched it in midair with catlike reflexes. "Hey, girl. The truth hurts…Listen, he probably swapped plates with his dead ex-wife, knowing that nobody was gonna report it. Hell, most jamokes don't even know their own tag number, unless it's a personalized plate."

"We could check with places that do vinyl lettering and logos. Might get a lead on where he lives."

"Good thinkin', Pard, but my hunch is he probably bought all the computer equipment to do the work himself. Used a fake name and a temporary address…Would lead us exactly nowhere, after a whole lot of legwork." He frowned.

Loraine mulled his response over. "So, where does that leave us now?"

"Back to my original hypothesis. He's out for revenge for the major hose job he received in that divorce."

"Gotta point there, big guy. That was a really lopsided judgment."

"Yep. If that was my settlement, both attorneys would be on the hit list as well."

"Yeah, I wouldn't want to be in their shoes, either." She shook her head and sighed. "What are we gonna do about it?"

Bone stood up quickly. "Come on, woman. Gotta sell this kettle of fish to St. John."

GAINESVILLE MUNICIPAL BUILDING

Stella pulled into one of the half-dozen parking spots along South Rusk Street facing the single story, red brick building that housed several city offices. She and Juan climbed out and quickly entered the west doors near the City Manager's office. They turned left and entered the first door to their left.

The forty-year old receptionist was her usual friendly self. She smiled and spoke directly to Stella. "Howdy, y'all. How may I help you?"

"Morning, Rita. We need to speak with Steve. Have a little issue with CPS."

Rita's smile melted away. "Sorry to hear that. You know, this is the third complaint we're heard since we hired the new manager there."

She checked her computer screen to review the man's schedule. Fortunately, in a small town like Gainesville, population of only 16,000, the daily demands on a city manager were not overwhelming.

"Go on in...His next appointment isn't until eleven."

Steve Schmidt, a thirty-four year old professional with a master's degree in city planning and public administration was seated in a moderate-sized office adjoining his receptionist.

He rose when Stella and Juan walked in. "Hi, guys, have a seat." He looked at Juan. "You might want to close that door." He pointed to the one between his office and Rita's.

Juan did as he was suggested, and then joined Stella standing next to a pair of chairs opposite Steve's mahogany desk.

The City Manager looked directly at Stella. "Good job on that homicide yesterday, Corporal Johnson. Thank God, we don't have many of those in this town."

"Thank you, sir, my partner here was a big part in that." She turned to her rookie trainee. "Juan, shake hands with Steve Schmidt...Steve, patrolman Juan Gomez, our latest addition to the PD."

The two men greeted each other.

"Pleasure to meet you, sir," Juan said.

Steve smiled as he said, "The pleasure is all mine. The chief filled me in on yesterday's activities. I must say I was impressed...Sit down and tell me what's up...Heard something about an issue over at CPS." His face became serious as he settled down in his high backed office chair.

Stella and Juan took a seat. She laid the Barbie on the executive's desk. "You got the info about the little abandoned three-year old girl who became an orphan yesterday...Found that in her family's car and wanted to get it to her..." Her golden eyes were somewhat cold as she gazed down at it.

"Anyway, we had a little break and stopped by CPS to give it to her and have Juan translate what I needed to tell her about her mom and all."

Steve nodded and said, "Go on."

"Well, Jabba the Hut working the desk over there wouldn't let us see her without the manager's approval."

"That's not out of line in such a case, I suppose."

Juan interrupted. "But, Latoya Washington, the huge woman at the CPS desk said the manager was at lunch and wouldn't be back until 1:30 or 2:00. Who takes four hour lunches?"

Steve frowned. "That doesn't exactly sound like great customer service. I haven't met this Latoya at this point...Maria Conseco, the new CPS manager brought her on board."

Stella spoke up, "Another thing that I thought was odd was the woman wouldn't tell us where Carmen was at this time. That sent a alarm flag for me. Something is not quite right and I can't put my finger on it."

Steve ran his left index finger over his lower lip as he listened to the two cops. "This concerns me... As Rita said, this is the third complaint we've heard about that office...I tend to trust your judgment over that of a distraught relative who is in the middle of a child custody issue. Those can get really emotional and nasty…as you are probably aware."

"Tell me about it," Stella said with a slight laugh.

"Okay, gang. I've got time…Let's go over to CPS and see if we can get this worked out in person. I hate those paper chases that sometimes get out of hand when a little direct action can nip it…"

"In the bud." Juan stuck out his fist.

Steve grinned and gave him a fist bump.

§

CHAPTER THIRTEEN

GAINESVILLE POLICE DEPARTMENT

Captain St. John stared at him with a look of disgust. "Bone, that's about the biggest load of horse crap you've ever tried to shovel past me. You must think I'm some kind of idiot to buy all that scientific mumbo jumbo."

Loraine looked at Bone and shrugged.

Bone shook his head. "Listen, Cap'n. You know me. I like to bend the rules sometimes…"

"Sometimes? Try all of the time." His eyes narrowed.

"What I mean to say is, this is not one of my little practical jokes…I know you don't savvy the technical lingo I told you about infrasonic, harmonic resonance, extremely low-frequency stuff."

He held up his right hand as if he was swearing an oath. "Honest, I did actually call one of my other old Marine commanders, you remember Major Martine, now Colonel…who confirmed they have sonic weapons in development…Look, Cap'n, I'm not just trying to get out of the office for a few hours…It's too damn hot to fish, anyway."

The captain scowled.

Loraine watched as the thought of the whole operation becoming a no-go floated past. "Hey Captain. Look at this case as a simple revenge deal. Man gets screwed big time in a divorce and man gets even…Can you see that angle?"

He eyeballed her coldly. "Makes more sense than a Buck Rogers ray gun that can scramble your

146

brain and rip out your heart without leaving a mark."

"Yeah, that's the other part of this deal." Bone glanced at Loraine and gave her a quick nod.

"What all do you need…if I do get stupid and let you do this?" St. John folded his arms and placed his elbows on his desk, leaning toward Bone.

"Just a couple T ac guys and another two units to run down potential vics. My partner and I can't be everywhere at once."

"Dammit, Bone, you know what the chief thinks about overtime?" He considered his options. "All right, you big lug. You got three days. Three…" He held up three fingers and then pointed his index finger at Bone's chest. "…and if you get any of my people killed…don't bother comin' back. Understand?"

"Got it, Cap'n. Come on, Pard. Let's vamoose before he changes his mind." He stood up and grinned. "Laterbye."

They hurried out of their supervisor's office. Once several feet down the hall, Bone turned to Loraine. He gave her a thumbs up and then held up an open hand for a high five.

She slapped at it, only to miss when Bone's arm shot straight up almost to the dropped ceiling.

"You were this close," he said with a huge grin. He held his thumb and index finger about one inch apart.

"Don't make me jump, you egotistical jackass." She made a fist and pointed at his crotch. "How'd you like your huevos scrambled?"

"Ooh…Think I'll pass, ninja shortcakes."

"See? That's why you had trouble swaying the Cap'n…he's seen too much of your crap for too many years. I saved your butt, Bone…Might as well admit it, Jackalope.."

"Okay, possibly…maybe. We'll never know for sure. Sometimes the bossman takes a little time to see the brilliance of my plans."

"Low bridge…duck." She pointed upward.

Bone ducked and looked up and then all around. His face displayed his confusion. "What?"

"Your ego is swelling your pointed little head so much, I was truly afraid you wouldn't make it through the door way." She threw him a fake smile.

"All right, princess. How 'bout a truce? At least until we get a team together."

"Deal."

They continued down the hall to the Tactical Operations section.

GAINESVILLE CPS OFFICES

Stella whipped into the reserved parking space and shut down the patrol unit. Two other privately owned cars were parked in adjacent spaces. She and her partner exited and Juan opened the back seat to allow the city manager to climb out.

Steve had a somewhat sheepish grin on his face. "First time for a ride in the back seat of one of our police units. Didn't realize that there were no door handles on the inside."

Juan laughed. "Most of our passengers are not there voluntarily. Works better for us if they can't get out."

Stella chuckled. "Besides, frequent riding in the back of a patrol car is not exactly a resume builder, if you catch my drift."

Steve nodded. "Let's see if we can get this little misunderstanding ironed out."

The three entered the front door. Latoya was once again at her desk, but Stella noted there was no one else in the reception area.

Steve approached the desk. "Hi, I'm Steve Schmidt, the City Manager. Don't believe we've met." He extended his hand.

Latoya sat with her arms folded over her more than ample belly. "We have now. Whatch'all want?"

The surprised executive glanced at Stella. She said nothing but gave him a look that said *I told you so* loud and clear.

Steve recovered quickly. "We'd like to see Carmen Santiago, *now*." His tone left no question about his intentions.

Latoya doubled down on stupid. "You think this is Burger King? You cain't have it your way over to here." She pointed a chubby finger at Stella and then Juan. "I done tol' these two they cain't see the little girl without permission from my supervisor. And I don't know you from Jack Robinson." She glared at the City Manager and pursed her lips.

Steve's ears turned a tinge of red as his blood pressure began to rise. "Miss Washington, you are subject to termination for insubordination. I have two credible witnesses to your actions."

"You don't scare me, white boy. I knows my rights and I gots me a good lawyer I can call. You cain't fire me, cause I'm black." She jutted her chin out.

Stella sensed something was wrong—very wrong. "Steve, with your permission, I'm going to search the premises. I got a bad feeling about this place." Her hand was resting on the Glock 19 at her side.

"Go ahead," he said.

Latoya was fuming as she struggled to her feet. "You ain't goin' no where, honky bitch...I'm in charge here."

In the blink of an eye, Stella had the 9mm pointed at the three hundred pounder's head. "Back up! Keep your hands where I can see them." She glanced at Juan. He had his weapon drawn as well. "Keep her covered. Don't let her move a muscle."

Latoya's eyes were like two saucers.

"She's all mine, " Juan said. "Go find Carmen."

Steve was a bit unsure of what was happening. For the first time in his life he was lost for words.

Stella lowered her pistol to a low tactical as she headed down the narrow hallway. "You coming, Mister Schmidt?"

"Right behind you." He looked over his shoulder at the standoff in the reception area. *Oh man, this went south in a hurry.*

Stella came up to the first doorway on the left, a room on the street side of the building. She took in a deep breath, turned the door knob silently and then opened it quickly, not allowing the door to slam against the wall.

Inside the small room were a set of bunk beds and a single bed on the opposite side. Several donated stuffed animals were lying on the children friendly bed spreads.

Stella looked at Steve and shrugged. "About what I would expect."

"Uh huh."

She closed the door gently. Crossing the hall, she repeated the same entry technique on the door. But the sight that greeted her was one she would never forget.

A naked middle-aged Hispanic man was mounted atop a nude child who was bound spread-eagled hand and foot to the single bed. The tiny child's face was partially covered by a white cloth gag.

"Carmen! Get off her you sick bastard!"

Stella brought the gun up to shoulder height as she squared off facing him.

BONE'S PARADOX

The man rolled off of the young girl and panicked when he saw the much smaller female police officer. He rushed at her with arms outstretched.

Three rapid shots rang out—but not nearly as loud as Stella had expected. The first clipped off the rapist's thumb on his out-stretched hand before digging into his sternum. The one-hundred-ninety pound man closed the distance even more as a second round pierced his heart and the third shot tore through his right eye and exited the back of his skull. His lifeless body collapsed forward onto her left leg, knocking her to the bedroom floor. "Get off me!" she yelled as a crimson pool of warm blood spread across the white tile.

Stella placed her right foot on the shoulder of the deceased man and forcefully kicked him off her pinned down leg. She sat up, her breathing coming in ragged shallow pants.

Schmidt was stunned by the sudden turn to violence. "Oh my God! Oh my God...What's going on?"

Juan called from down the hall. "Stella! You okay?" He eyeballed the suddenly extremely nervous Latoya Washington. His normally calm demeanor shifted to much more aggressive posture as his adrenaline kicked in. "Don't even think about it, woman. I'll drop you before you make it to the door."

Stella's voice came over the police radio. "Dispatch, Bravo 28."

Laurie noted the higher pitch to Stella's voice and the rapid cadence. "Bravo 28, Dispatch, go ahead."

"Dispatch, Bravo 28, shots fired...shots fired. Officer involved shooting. The suspect is down."

Laurie breathed a sigh of relief. "Dispatch roger suspect is down. Say your location."

"Child Protective Services building, uh...313 East Pecan Street."

"Dispatch roger CPS building, rolling EMS at this time. Do you require backup?"

Stella looked around the room. The walls and ceiling were covered with soundproofing foam and the window facing the alley was boarded up with heavy plywood. *Lord Jesus. This is a rape room.* "Bravo 28, affirmative. Backup required." She stumbled to her feet and rushed to the bed.

She struggled with the knot in the white cloth wrapped around Carmen's tiny head. "It's okay, baby girl, I'm here now..." The unseeing blank stare in the child's brown eyes stopped her cold.

As she lifted the gag from Carmen's mouth, the sight of dried vomit confirmed her worst fear. *Oh dear God. She's dead.*

§

CHAPTER FOURTEEN

GAINESVILLE POLICE STATION

Bone stepped into the Tactical Operations room, followed closely by Loraine. A well-muscled forty-year-old police sergeant had an AR-15 disassembled on his work bench and was cleaning the recesses of the bolt carrier with a stack of Q-tips and Hoppes powder solvent.

"Hey, Moomer. How's it hanging old buddy?"

The man looked up and grinned at Bone. "I may not be as good as I once was, but I'm as good once as I ever was." His voice reflected an unrepaired cleft palate. Because of his speech impediment, some folks made the mistake of thinking he wasn't very bright, but Bone and the rest of the department knew if you needed armed backup, there was no one better than Moomer.

"Glad to hear everything is still in working order," Bone said. "What would you say about a little tactical detail? Cap'n gave us the go ahead for three days."

"Music to my ears." Moomer's face lit up. "Whatcha need? The Barrett fifty? 300 Mag sniper rig or M-4s?"

"Might need all of the above. Seem like we got us a counter sniper situation brewin'…"

The Tactical Operations room had a handheld scanner on the Dispatch operational frequency at all times. Whenever a call came in that might involve hostages, high speed chases, or a barricaded suspect, being privy to the event from the time of initial notification saved much needed response time.

Moomer leaned over and turned up the volume on the transceiver when the shots fired call came in from Stella.

Loraine listened intently to the woman's voice. "Guys, Bravo 28 is Stella."

Bone gave her a look. "We know that, Pard. Where the hell is she?"

They listened for the next few transmissions. Loraine's face grew progressively more somber. "CPS?…Dammit. That's where they took that little abandoned girl yesterday. I wonder if she is somehow involved?" She searched Bone's face.

He shrugged. "Beats hell outta me. Can't tell a thing from here."

Two minutes passed. The call for backup and a an investigator was tinged with more emotion that all three picked up on.

"Stella doesn't sound too good if you ask me," Moomer observed.

Loraine nodded. "Bone, she needs some help, and I have to find out if Carmen is okay. Can we go?"

"You bet, Pard…Moom, sorry to leave you but…you know how it is. Put together three shooters and a variety of tactical gear…Both urban and rural capable. Fill you in when we get back."

"Okie dokie, but when do we need to assemble?"

Bone checked his watch. "Fourteen hundred. Be ready to roll."

Moomer grinned. "Can do easy."

By the time Bone's VW Thing turned onto East Pecan street, the CPS Office parking lot was full. Two other patrol SUVs and a pair of EMS ambulances had taken every available spot.

Bone pulled alongside the curb and parked across the street. He slapped a *Police Official Business* placard on the skinny dashboard and rested it against the steering wheel. "Joy to the world. Let the circus begin. Grab the CSI kit from the back seat, Pard."

"I got it." She stepped out and looked at all the vehicles. "Hope to hell they kept the scene somewhat sterile."

"Wishful thinkin'. The first five minutes are always the most chaotic."

Inside, Bone spotted Juan talking to a pair of other patrolmen. Latoya was seated in one of the stack-able chairs with her hands cuffed behind her back. Her face was a sea of rage.

Steve Schmidt was in a similar chair on the other side of the room talking on his cell phone.

Stella was behind the receptionist's desk. Her left sleeve was rolled up and one of the paramedics was taking a blood sample.

When the other patrolmen saw Bone and Loraine enter, the conversation dropped to almost nil.

Juan broke off from his conversation and approached the big man. "We cleared the building after the incident. Found another rape room on the far end." He pointed down the hall.

Bone's eyebrows arched. "Didn't hear 'bout that on the scanner. Good thing, too…Otherwise the media would have a field day with this goat rope." He pointed a thumb at Steve. "What's he doing here?"

"Official business…Stella and I went to his office to get some help with Jabba the Hut over there. All we wanted to do is give the little girl her doll."

"The unhappy camper over there denied us a visit. You'll see why when you enter the first room on the right."

"We'll get to that. Were you a direct witness?"

"No, sir, I was holding that one at gun point."

"Really? What was your probable cause?"

Juan blanched. "Uh...my partner pulled her weapon and told me to cover her."

"Stella did that?" Bone turned to look at the petite blonde. "Damn...had to be some kind of reason. She's not normally a hothead."

Loraine shook her head. "Doesn't sound like the Stella Johnson I know...not at all."

Juan shrugged. "You see, Latoya over there refused to let the City Manager see the girl, either. He threatened to fire her for insubordination...she doubled down and played the race card. Stella's gut instinct told her something was wrong...Bad wrong. That's when she drew her weapon."

"Always trust your gut," Bone said with conviction.

"Where's Carmen?" There was an urgency in Loraine's voice.

Tears welled up in Juan's eyes. For a moment he could not find the words. He wiped them clear and shook his head. "You don't want to see her that way."

Loraine gasped and covered her mouth.

Bone's caught sight of the anguish in his partner. His jaw took a hard set. "Where is she?...It's our job, Juan."

The rookie's voice cracked a little. "She's in the first room on the right." He wiped away another tear.

Bone took in a deep breath. "Hey, has anybody searched that Latoya for weapons?"

Juan shook his head. "Dammit, no...I thought it would be better if a woman handled the search and Stella was..." his voice trailed off.

Bone pointed a finger at Juan. "Listen up, rookie Never let traumatic events overcome protocol. If you don't have a female officer who can do a search, do whatever you need to make sure your prisoner is not armed. You can't let them out of your sight for a second until you verify that personally. Otherwise, you and you partner can both end up dead...*Sabe usted*?"

He turned to Loraine. "Pard, I need you to take Miss Congeniality over there into the office and pat her down properly. Have one of the other patrol officers stand by just outside the door...Just in case. Okay?"

She nodded. "I can do that." She turned and grabbed Latoya by the elbow. "Get up. We're gonna do a quick little search."

Latoya jerked her arm from Loraine. She made no effort to get to her feet. "Piss off, Mexican bitch. I ain't got to do nuthin' you say…I wanna talk to my lawyer."

Loraine smiled sardonically. She leaned in and whispered, "Woman, you don't really want to learn all the ways I can make you scream for mercy. I got seven black belts in Kung Fu that I'm itchin' to use in tunin' you up."

Latoya spit in her face. "I ain't scared of you, little britches."

Loraine wiped the spittle away. Her eyes glowed with fire. "Assault on a police officer. Strike two, three and you're out of here." She reached behind the woman and gabbed hold of a fat little finger and bent it backwards ninety degrees. "On your feet, tubby, if you want to ever be able to count to ten again."

Latoya let out a bloodcurdling scream and lunged to her feet. "Let go of my hand!"

Bone watched from a distance and grinned. *Big mistake to rile up Shortcakes.*

Loraine snatched hold of the prisoner's index finger and folded it back as well. She steered the woman away from the chair and pointed her towards the manager's office—lifting the huge woman's arms high behind her back.

"You're killing me!" Latoya screamed.

"Not yet...but the day's not over." Investigator Rodriguez was only half joking.

Bone watched until the two women disappeared into the office and Loraine closed the door. He noticed that the paramedic was done with the blood sample on Stella. He turned to Juan. "Excuse me, I need to speak with your partner."

He walked up beside her and sat down on the corner of the desk. His face showed compassion for a fellow cop. "Hey, little bit. Some day, huh?"

She nodded but said nothing.

"You doing okay?" He reached out for her hand. Taking it in one hand he placed his other on top of hers, completely dwarfing the petite corporal's gentle hand.

He closed his eyes for a second. Visions of the rape room filled his consciousness—the nude bound child, and her adult rapist. In slow motion he saw the man charging at him. A Glock came up to eye level and fired three times. He could see the severed thumb of the attacker fly over his right shoulder. The man's eye went dark, followed by bits of blood, bone and brain mater spraying out in a fan-shaped pattern. The image changed as the man crashed into him and he fell backwards to the floor.

Bone's body shook a tiny bit as he released contact with Stella.

She stared at him as his eyes opened and then seemed to focus again. "Guess I'm doing' all right, all things considered. Are you okay?"

"Sure, kid, couldn't be better…Just the stress of thinking about how tough things are for you, I suppose." He sighed at having to lie to a good friend. "Listen, you don't have to answer any of my questions if you don't want to…Officer involved shootings are handled just like homicides. You have a right to an attorney…"

"Cut the crap, Bone…I know the drill. It was a legit shooting. The murdering bastard attacked me."

"I know…Believe me I know. I'll get into the scene in a few minutes…It ain't going anywhere."

Stella's eyes filled with tears. "I'm glad you're the one doing the investigation. Know you'll do it right." She looked down the hall. "I just wanted little Carmen to have her doll." Tears flowed down her face taking some mascara with them.

Bone's eyes misted over, too. "I know, baby girl. That's the kind of person you are." He dabbed at his eyes. "Sounds like these animals were using CPS for some sicko kiddie sex slave crap."

She nodded. "I could sense something was wrong. Didn't know what..." She tried to choke back a sob. "I let little Carmen down. She's dead because of me...Me, Bone!" Stella looked up at him with tear filled eyes and a quivering lower lip.

Bone wrapped his arms around her and pulled her close to him. "No, Baby, that's not so. You did everything right and decent and loving." A single crystal-clear tear ran down his left cheek and dropped into her golden hair. He took in a deep breath trying to pull in his own emotions. "Sometimes...sometimes things happen that are outside our control. Don't know why God lets the devil have free rein down here."

He hugged her tightly for a few more seconds and released her. He lifted her chin with his huge hand. "I'll do my dead level best to get the forensics that will prove you acted in self defense...You just gotta trust me." He kissed her forehead.

Stella wiped away her eyes on the back of her hand. "I do, you big ox…I trust you with my life."

§

CHAPTER FIFTEEN

GAINESVILLE CPS OFFICE

All the other police personnel had departed the premises. EMS had removed the bodies to the morgue for autopsy. Latoya Washington was not enjoying her stay in the Cooke County lockup. Bone and Loraine were putting away the last of the crime scene samples into the CSI kit. He looked at his watch. "Dang it. No wonder I'm starving…It's one-twenty already."

His partner look at him in disgust. "How could you possible eat after seeing all that gore?…I won't be able to eat for a week."

"Look, I only had a burrito for breakfast. There's only like fifteen calories in one of those."

"Poor baby…Suppose we could run by Braums before we head back to meet Moomer. Wouldn't want you to dry up and blow away…You 'ittle bitty thing." She gave him another one of her fake smiles.

"All right…have your fun, but when your blood sugar drops like a prom dress in a limousine…"

Suddenly from the front of the building, a woman's voice called out, "Latoya? Where the hell are you? I brought some more clients."

Bone looked at Loraine. "Do you think?" he whispered.

She shrugged and whispered back, "Maria Canseco, the female manager that Steve told us about?"

"Possible. There's no sign up front what happened back here. Maybe she doesn't know."

The pair drew their weapons as the voice came closer.

"Latoya, you better not be sleeping on duty…"

A forty year old Hispanic woman dressed in a gaudy orange pantsuit opened the closed door to the bedroom across the hall. She slammed it when her search was unsuccessful. "Latoya! Get you butt out here, woman."

She stepped into the doorway of the first rape room, and froze at the sight of a Kimber .45 and Smith and Wesson .500 leveled at her. She raised her hands.

"Maria Conseco, I presume?" Loraine stepped closer.

"Yes, uh, I mean no…I've never been here before in my life." She looked back over her shoulder at three scruffy looking men who had followed her down the hallway. "I don't know these men or what they are doing here."

Bone chuckled. "And I'm Santa Claus…You're under arrest for kidnapping, sex trafficking, organized criminal conspiracy and murder."

The color ran from Maria's face.

BONE'S PARADOX

GAINESVILLE POLICE STATION

Loraine escorted the newest prisoner from booking to the north doors. Outside, two patrol officers took over and placed her in the back seat of their four door sedan for transport to the Cooke County jail.

Bone joined then and handed over a manila folder with printouts of her criminal charges, past rap sheet and a large see-through plastic bag filled with her personal items.

"Here you go, Joel." He chuckled. "Miss Canseco almost meets the dress code for the steel motel already."

Officer Newman shook his head. "Can't believe you lucky suckers took her down so easily. If she had gotten wind her little empire was already busted, we'd have never gotten her out of Mexico."

Loraine agreed. "Rather be lucky than good, right Pard?"

"Nah, I like good...great...extraordinary is even better."

Loraine took one look at his smug face. "Honest to Pete...Joel, see what I have to put up with?"

He grinned. ""Yes, Ma'am...He's a legend in his own mind." He stuck out a fist and Bone bumped it.

"And don't you ever forget it either…Laterbye." He wheeled around and headed for the doors.

Loraine threw up her hands in frustration and followed along behind. She had barely entered the building when she stumbled into Bone talking to Captain St. John.

The senior officer had his arms crossed in front of his chest. Loraine's first impression was *Oh no…what did Bone do to piss off the old man?*

"I was just down at the operations center and I find out you were not on your Buck Rogers death ray mission that just this morning I had begrudgingly approved. Is that correct?" St. John sounded more than a little irritated.

Loraine eased up beside Bone to take her medicine.

"Well boss, it's like this…"

The Captain cut him off. "Stop…Don't want to hear it." He looked at Loraine. "I send both of you out on a harebrained project and you drop it like a hot potato to put yourself in the middle of an officer involved shooting."

Bone gave a side glance to his partner. "But Stella…"

St. John held up his hand and shook his index finger in front of Bone face. "Not a word. Did either of you give a minute's thought as to how much paper work and forensics are involved in such a case?"

Bone and Loraine both shook their heads.

"Then, even as you were finishing the unassigned CSI, the ringleader of the nefarious evil mess falls in your lap and you sack her up like a bag of taters...Does that about cover it?"

Bone shrugged. "Yeah, pretty much."

Loraine nodded. "Guess you could say that."

St. John frowned. "I've been thinking about how many days it's gonna take you two to write up the forensic report proving Corporal Johnson was in fear for her life." He looked at this watch. "You guys are supposed to meet Moomer and your Tac team in fifteen minutes. Is that Charlie?"

"Affirmative, Cap'n." Bone straightened up a bit.

St. John's face was serious as a heart attack. "You know, part of me thinks another lawyer or two pushin' up daisies would not be such a bad thing...But then there's that part that signed up to promote law and order...It says we gotta stop that homicidal maniac from killing a few more shysters…Tell me how I can help you."

Bone rubbed his stomach. "Well, Boss, we kinda worked straight through our lunch hour. Think you could you run over to Braum's for us?"

Loraine's jaw dropped. *Bone are you nuts? Can't friggin' believe you asked him that.*

"Double meat cheeseburger, mustard, add jalapenos, no onions…Super size the fries and a jumbo chocolate shake?"

"Right, Cap'n," Bone grinned. "You know what I like. Hold the phone…On second thought, better make it a triple. We might run a little late tonight."

"You got it." St. John glanced at Loraine. "How 'bout you, Shortcakes? You hungry, too?"

"No, I…uh…wait, maybe a grilled chicken on whole wheat, mayo, cut the onions and ice tea?"

"No fries?" St. John asked.

She shook her head. "I'll steal some of Bone's."

"You bet." The stocky captain turned to leave, but quickly spun around. "Come back with your shields or on them…Semper Fi, you two." He gave them a thumbs up, wheeled and walked away quickly.

Loraine's shoulder slumped. She stared up at Bone, not quite sure of what had occurred. "What the hell just happened? Is he really buying us lunch?"

Bone chuckled. "Yep. It's his way of sayin' job well-done...Marine style."

"Holy crap. Thought he was gonna suspend us or something."

Bone put his arm around her shoulder. "Not a chance. We made the department look good and him look good...He's a seriously happy camper."

"Yeah? Would be great if he let his face know."

"Not his MO. But you must be growing on him. He called you Shortcakes."

Loraine did a double take. "Oh my God...He did. That dirty bird."

Bone smiled. "Chill out, Double D, we still have a lot of work to do. Let's see what Moomer has put together in the meantime."

"Damn you, Bone!"

Stella Johnson knocked twice on Chief Anderson's office door. She heard "Come on in," from the other side. She had changed out of her bloodstained pants and into a backup pair she kept in her locker. A few minutes spent washing off her face and applying new makeup and mascara had removed most of the visible signs of the traumatic morning. Stella took in a deep breath and opened the door.

Chief Anderson, a thirty-five year veteran of law enforcement sat behind a large cherry wood executive desk. The walls were covered with plaques of commendations, training certificate, degrees as well as an assortment of professional and personal photos. His hair was gray, cut short and receding at the temples. He removed his wire-rimmed readers and set them on his desk.

She entered, closing the door behind her and walked to the middle of the room. She stood at attention in front of his desk. "Corporal Johnson reporting as ordered."

"Have a seat, Stella."

"Thank you, sir." She sat down in a high-backed gray leather swivel based chair. His lips were pursed tightly.

"I understand you shot an unarmed man found having sex with a deceased minor child."

"Yes, sir." She cringed at the ominous sound of the term *unarmed man*. Oh, God…Here it comes.

"The individual you shot was reported to be dead at the scene."

"Yes, sir, that is also correct."

"In accordance with departmental policy, you will be placed on administrative leave...pending grand jury presentation and deliberation."

"I am familiar with departmental policy, sir."

"Stella, I am required to inform you that during that time, you will not be allowed to wear a uniform of this department, nor will you be able to act as a commissioned police officer while on such leave."

She nodded as he continued.

"You are probably aware as the potential adverse public outcry stemming from a shooting of an unarmed suspect...The news media is sure to make front page headlines of it."

"I have seen such things occur recently," Stella said in a low voice. *Can't believe this is happening to me. Why did that sick bastard have to attack me when I was looking for Carmen? My picture might be plastered on CNN. Dang it, I hate fake news.*

"I will authorize the payment of your usual salary during this period, unless the grand jury returns a true bill, in which case your administrative leave will become an administrative suspension, subject to termination."

Oh my God, can it get any worse? "Chief, I was in fear for my life. The man was attacking…"

He cut her off. "Corporal Johnson, you don't have to convince me…Besides, I haven't even seen the investigative report at this time. I'll need for you to leave your duty weapon, badge and ID here on the desk."

Stella was stunned for a moment. She stood up slowly, drew her Glock from its holster and laid it on the desk. The lanyard from her ID badge hung up on her pony tail for a couple of seconds. She turned her head, shook it free and laid it down beside the pistol. Lastly she reached up and flipped the safety catch on her gold shield shaped GPD badge pinned on her uniform blouse. Once it was free, she placed the badge pin in its V shaped cradle and rolled the tiny locking mechanism back in place. The sight of her police paraphernalia on his desk was seared into her memory.

§

CHAPTER SIXTEEN

GAINESVILLE POLICE DEPARTMENT

Bone stopped short of the hallway to the Tactical Section. "Hey, Pard, if you need to hit the ladies room, now's as good a time as any...Gotta grab something from my desk, anyway."

"Sounds good to me. Meet you there." She turned left toward the rest rooms while Bone quickly went to his office.

He pulled out his lower desk drawer and grabbed three oversized speed loaders. Each contained five rounds of his .500 Smith and Wesson ammunition and was contained in a tan-colored saddle leather belt pouch. Two loaders had Barnes 275 grain solid copper hollowpoint projectiles, while the third was designed specifically to knock out vehicle engines and transmissions. A whopping 400 grains of nickel-plated tungsten steel could punch through a truck's bumper or frame, then smash a hole through both sides of the engine block and keep on going.

"Twenty five rounds oughta do," Bone muttered as he hung the carriers on his Ranger-style duty belt and clicked the nickel-plated brass snaps shut. He adjusted the fit where he liked them—two with hollowpoints forward on his left hip and the heavy hitting armor piercing 400 grain in front of his everyday lighter Barnes solid copper fare.

From his top drawer, he opened a clamshell eyeglass case and pulled out a pair of mirror finished version of his Bausch and Lomb oversized aviator glasses. He swapped them with the dark green polarized ones in his right front shirt pocket.

He removed a heavy manila folder from his upper left hand drawer and headed out.

Loraine took a seat on a stool next to Sergeant Moomer Martin. Three other Tactical Team shooters were seated nearby. "Where's Conan?" asked former USAF Air Policeman, Rick Gore.

"He'll be here in a minute or so. We left the info about the trial judges in the office."

Mike Spencer, another Marine combat veteran, was also curious. "Can you give a little hint about what this little caper is all about? Moom didn't know jack."

"Just a revenge deal, far as we can make out. The suspect is a real whiz kid…"

"With a severely bent beak," Bone said as he made his entrance. "Our guy lost four point two mil in a lopsided divorce settlement…We believe he offed the trial judge, his ex-trophy wife, and her boy toy."

"Wow," Moomer said with wide eyes. "That's a lotta reasons to get your nose outta joint." He put his finger against his left nostril and pushed it to the side.

Rick laughed. "Moom always wanted to be a comedian.

Bone grinned. "Vaudeville's loss." He flopped the manilla folder open on the desk, took color prints of the suspect and passed them around. "We have here one Philip Kent Knight, male Caucasian, age thirty-nine…Slim build, maybe weighs one sixty in his BVDs…Stands six foot tall, and may or may not have the pony tail and facial hair he did at the second murder scene."

Moomer looked a bit confused. "Y'all got security footage of him at the scene?"

Bone and Loraine exchanged looks. She grinned. "We actually got to meet him…He called the last two deaths in to 911."

"Why didn't you take him into custody then and there?" Rick inquired.

"Good question," Bone replied. "Tell the young man why, Pard."

"Mister Knight was using the disguise of Philip Kent, pool man…at the home he lost to his ex."

Mike Spencer sat back in his chair. "Gutsyest move I ever saw, Mav...Damn, that takes some serious balls."

"Or, just a world class cold-blooded psychopath, slash narcissist," Bone said. "In any event, we're not here to do a psych eval on the dude." He picked up the sheets with the contact info on the three lawyers involved in the divorce case. "Okay, how are you guys paired up?"

Moomer raised his hand. He pointed at Rick. "He and I are Tac Team Two...Spencer and Mad Max will answer to Team Three. Since you called this rodeo...you be Team One."

Bone nodded. "Simple enough. He handed a contact information sheet on attorney Carl Spears to Moomer. "The deceased plaintiff in the divorce proceedings hired two lawyers. You get this one. Call his office and check his schedule. I want you two to stick on him like ticks on hound dog."

He took another sheet and handed it to Mad Max Maxwell. "You and Mike have co-council Winston Lyons. Same deal as with Spears...Loraine and I will take the poor SOB who lost the case for Philip Knight...Jimmy Jack Johnson."

"Lucky you," said Mad Max with a grim smile.

Bone shrugged. "Tell the truth, I don't have a clue who ol' Phil hates the most. My partner and I didn't get a chance to run down the details earlier due the major cluster down at CPS this mornin'…Get on the phone and start with the shylock's schedules. Gotta locate 'em first to bird dog 'em."

By the time the initial calls were completed, it was apparent that Jimmy Jack was in court on another civil case. Spears and Lyons had a 2:45 tee time at the Gainesville Municipal Golf Course.

St. John walked in with two takeout sacks from Braum's. "Here you go, guys. Never let it be said your captain let you go hungry." He handed the sacks to Bone and Loraine. "Need anything else?"

Bone shook his head. "Nah. That'll do for now."

Loraine opened her sack lunch. "Thanks Cap'n."

St. John nodded. "Good luck guys…and gal."

He walked out of the room without another word.

Rick looked hard at Bone. "You got pictures of him and a dog or somethin'? He never brought me lunch."

Moomer chimed in, "Me neither."

Bone unwrapped his triple patty, full pound of Texas beef cheeseburger. His smile was genuine. "Me and the Cap'n go way back."

He took a bite and while he chewed it, spread out the paper wrapper and dumped a humongous load of still warm french fries from a paper container.

Loraine took a bite of her chicken sandwich. She grabbed a small packet of mustard and spread the contents on the corner of Bone's burger wrapper. She dipped a golden fry in the yellow condiment and took a bite.

"Philistine," Bone said as he frowned. "Mustard is for hotdogs...Fries cry out for catsup."

The other Tac Team officers shared glances with each other.

Moomer waited until Bone had eaten half his gigantic burger and had started on his chocolate shake. "I hate to interrupt, but we really need to get going if we're gonna meet those guys before they tee off."

Bone wiped his mouth with a paper napkin. "By all means. Don't wait on me...Court doesn't recess until 4:00 ."

"Gear up, boys," Moomer said to the others.

All four men grabbed their fully-loaded, level four armor plate carriers, with extra mags, pistols, and comm gear attached to Mollie webbing. They lifted them over their heads and began to snug the cumberbuns containing soft level three side plates.

Bone dredged several fries through a puddle of catsup and popped them in his mouth. He chewed them quickly and washed them down with a sip of malt. "Uh…guys, one more thing."

Moomer picked up the suppressed, scoped, M-14 rifle in a black zippered tactical case and turned around. "What's that, Bone meister?"

"Y'all don't need all that heavy body armor."

"What do you mean?" asked Rick.

Bone set his burger down. "I forgot to tell you…it won't do any good against whatever Knight is using."

Mad Max moved in closer. "What the hell is he using that can defeat level four armor? A fifty BMG?"

Bone shook his head. "When I find out, we'll both know. All I can say is, if you get a shot at Phil Knight, take it…you might not get another chance."

You could have heard a pin drop.

§

CHAPTER SEVENTEEN

GAINESVILLE GOLF COURSE

Moomer Martin drove the GPD tactical Surburban to the golf course parking lot next to the clubhouse. He pulled into a spot near the main entrance and stepped out with a pair of twelve power Steiner binoculars.

He scanned the area, as Team Three pulled into the lot in a Chevy Tahoe SUV.

Corporal Rick Gore disembarked the vehicle and lifted his scope-equipped Remington 700 rifle out of a hard Pelican case from in the back seat. He cycled the bolt, driving a 7.62x51 round into the chamber and then thumbed the safety on. "See anything suspicious, Moom?"

"Negative on that," he replied without taking the optics from his eyes.

He scanned the tree line along the eighteenth green. *Nothing out of the ordinary*. He turned toward the practice range. Three men were warming up and hitting range balls at a few distance marking sign posts.

Moomer called to Corporal Maxwell, "From the photo on his driver's license, I'd say your boy is the one in the jade-colored polo shirt over there at the practice tees."

Mad Max glanced that direction. "Can't ID him for sure from here."

"I'll check it out," said Sergeant Mike Spencer. "Can you clear the clubhouse? Take Gore with you. Shouldn't take long...Looks pretty deserted at this time of day."

"Absolutely...Hotter'n a fire cracker out here in the sun...Pasture pool and heat stroke. Count me out." Max gave hand signals to Rick directing him to follow him into the building.

All the while, the four officers kept their heads on a swivel, looking for signs of Knight.

Spencer hung a Colt M-4 on a nylon sling over his neck and right shoulder. Keeping it at the low ready position—he approached the three golfers.

Winston Lyons teed up his ball and took a mighty swing. Unfortunately, he took his eye off the ball and topped it—sending it screaming along the ground as it clipped the top of the grass.

"Nice one, Winn," one of his foursome called out. "You call that a weed whacker or gopher getter?"

"Bite me, Elliot. I'm just gettin' warmed up."

"Gotta keep your head down, counselor," Mike said from a few yards away.

"Oh, yeah? Says who?" He spun around to face a heavily laden policeman in full tactical gear. "Oh... Afternoon officer...Uh...It wasn't me, I wasn't there, and I have witnesses will say that they did it." He pointed at his buddies and grinned.

"Winston Lyons?" the officer asked.

"That's what it says on the birth certificate, but friends just call me Winn." He transferred the Big Bertha to his left hand and stuck out his right.

Mike checked around the area quickly and then shook his hand. "Corporal Spencer, Gainesville PD...Sir, we have reason to believe your life might be in danger."

"Seriously? Has someone called in a threat?"

"Three people are dead...all connected to a recent divorce case you were involved with."

The color drained from Winn's face. "I heard Judge Lockhart had died suddenly...Who else?"

"Brittany Wilson Knight and her boyfriend."

"I hadn't heard that. When?"

"Yesterday." Spencer checked his watch. "Isn't Carl Spears supposed to be playing with you?"

Winn appeared close to becoming sick. He nodded. "Sure and he's usually very punctual." He looked at his two friends who had stopped practicing and had moved closer to catch the conversation.

"Don't suppose you have a cell number for him?...We tried his home, but it went to voice mail."

"Sure," Winn replied. "I'll buzz him and give him a heads-up."

He pulled a phone from his Bermuda shorts and made the call. After ten rings it went to voice mail. Concern was etched on the lawyer's face.

"Hey, Carl...Winn here. Give me a call, ASAP. It's important." He looked at the policeman and shook his head.

"Was afraid of that." Mike pulled the tactical radio off of his vest. "Team One, Team Three."

Bone answered quickly into his tiny boom mike attached to a custom-fitted ear bud. "Team Three, Team One...go."

"Team one, be advised that Spears is a no-show at his tee time. Have Lyons under our security. Negative contact on Spears' cell phone."

Bone pounded his fist on the dash of the brown wrapper—the unmarked police car he opted for rather than his personal VW Thing. *Dammit. Don't like the sound of this. Not one bit.*

Loraine watched intently as Bone's gold-flecked eyes narrowed.

"Team Two, Tac One."

Moomer grabbed his handheld. "Team Two is up."

"Team Two, proceed to 557 West Wyndemere Lane. Check on Spears' residence. Proceed with caution...over."

"Team Two, WILCO."

"Team Three, Team One."

"Team Three is with you."

"Copy, Team Three...Hunker down with assignee. Stay indoors...away from windows until further advised...Over."

Mike glanced at the shaken attorney. "Team Three, roger all." He hung the radio back on his Molle gear and looked at the rest of the golfers. "Sorry guys, but your game in postponed until we find out what's going on."

COOKE COUNTY COURTHOUSE

Bone whipped the tan Toyota into an available parking spot on the east side of the building. He killed the ignition and pulled the key.

"What's the plan, big guy? Wanna get all the hardware out of the trunk?"

"No, Ma'am. No need for the long guns...yet. There's not a shot over seventy-five yards on the square. Either one of us can handle that without side arms."

"If we can see him…maybe."

"Come on, Pard…He can't be invisible." Bone grinned, but the grin faded quickly. "At least I don't think so…Unless he's got one of these bracelets like Lucy gave me." He held his wrist up and dangled a turquoise and gold beaded alien artifact.

"Have you considered using it?"

"Only all the time. Actually, it works great for clandestine operations, and when you want to get away…Not ideal for executive protection."

"Why's that?" Loraine asked.

He held up his index finger. "In the first place, I don't want everybody and their dog knowing I have it…The NSA would send somebody to demand I give it up or steal it outright."

"You don't trust them?"

He chuckled. "Double D, hell, I don't even trust me."

"What's the second reason?"

"You are not a Marine…Wouldn't understand."

"Try me, Conan."

He smiled at her little dig. "When you don't know where the enemy is, you don't hide and wait...You send out someone to draw fire."

"Sounds like a good way to get yourself killed."

"Nobody gets to live forever...At least you get a Purple Heart."

She frowned and shook her head. "Do you think Spears is still alive?"

"Beats me...Never met the man. Moomer should get there within five minutes or less. We'll find out, soon enough. Let's mosey upstairs to the District Court and check on Jimmy Jack."

Bone glanced for oncoming traffic coming from behind and opened the car door. Stepping outside, he scanned the rooftops of the adjoining buildings in the historic downtown. He then checked out the windows in the oversized domed clock tower that effectively doubled the overall height of the court house. All four quadrants of the tower sported a large clock face which could be read from across the street. *Good place for a sniper*.

Loraine got out and scrutinized the area.

Both of them were on high alert as they climbed the broad steps up to the courthouse.

Bone stepped off the elevator and quickly scanned the balcony area of the fourth floor to the left. His hand was curled around the grip of his holstered .500 Smith and Wesson.

Loraine came out almost simultaneously and checked out the area to her right. There was not a single soul visible in either direction.

"Must still be in session," Bone said as he gazed across the open atrium, spotting no one whatsoever on that floor.

"The district court room is on the north side." Loraine said as she pointed toward a metal detector outside the entrance.

"Thanks for pointing that out, Cinderella. I've never been in this building before." His slightly sarcastic tone didn't go unnoticed.

"My bad…Just trying to help. You have a lot of things on your mind."

"The first of which is…Sometimes I hate it when I'm right."

"We don't know for certain that Spears is in jeopardy."

Bone turned around and gave her a grin. "Wanna bet another six pack of Shiner Bock on that?"

Loraine shook her head.

"You're learnin', Pard. You're learnin'."

He walked through the metal detector and noted it was turned off. He took hold of the polished brass handle on the massive door leading to the courtroom and gently opened it a few inches. He could see a sparse gallery crowd and two men seated at one table. Next to them was another table with a woman seated alone. A well-dressed woman who appeared to be her attorney was standing, addressing the judge. Bone closed the door silently.

"What's happening in there?" Loraine inquired.

"Our man Jimmy Jack is most likely defending some unlucky guy who's splittin' the sheets," he replied in a low voice. "We can wait out here until they recess...Didn't see anybody who could be Knight in the gallery."

They walked a few feet away where they could spot anyone coming up the stairs or exiting the elevator.

Just then, a call came through the ear buds that Bone and Loraine were wearing. "Team One, Team Two."

Bone glanced at her, raising his eyebrows. "Team One here. Whatcha got?"

BONE'S PARADOX

SPEARS RESIDENCE

Moomer kept a lookout for movement in the area as Rick Gore rolled the dead body over.

"Team One, be advised that Carl Spears will be permanently late for all future tee times. We found him face down beside his car with the trunk open and his clubs lying on the driveway."

Damn it. I knew it. Bone's jaw tightened visibly. "Any visible injury or sign of foul play?"

"Plenty of blood on the concrete...no signs of lacerations." He moved in closer. "Blood from the nose, mouth and...Holy crap! Even his eyes are bleedin'." He stepped back and swept the area with his M-4 rifle once more. He could feel the adrenaline kick in.

"Copy that," Bone replied. "I need you two to cover the east and south sides of the courthouse, pronto. Loraine and I will take the north and west. Court is still in session, and they usually shut down at four."

"Or when the judge says so," Loraine added.

"Tac Two, roger. We're en route now. I'll have Mad Max come in and secure the Spears murder scene."

"Tac One copies. Good call. Radio when you guys are in position."

"Tac Two, roger."

Loraine locked eyes with Bone. "You don't think Knight will try again today, do you?"

"Dunno. How much of a psychopath is he?"

Loraine felt the sweat building in her palms. She took in a deep breath and let it out slowly.

§

CHAPTER EIGHTEEN

WEST ELM STREET

A white Ford panel truck pulled into an empty curbside parking spot in the 100 block opposite the Cooke County Tax Appraisal building. Pristine new decals identified the van as a service vehicle for the Nortex-Texomaland cable TV system. A slender man in a tan company uniform stepped out and pulled a heavy brown web utility belt around himself and fastened the bayonet clasp in front with an audible click. He slipped a pair of leather gloves on, and then opened the sliding side door and removed two items. One was an olive drab painted metal tool box, the other a longer black case resembling one used by musicians to transport a trombone.

He looked both ways before crossing the street. There was next to no traffic on the side street one block north of the courthouse. Most folks were inside enjoying their air conditioning.

After traversing the deserted roadway, the man continued through the small parking lot behind the two-story office building. He nonchalantly started up the steel fire escape stairs and climbed both floors in less than forty-five seconds. When he reached the top landing, he sat the black case down for a moment as he pulled a nylon web strap from a pouch in his tool belt. Threading one end of it through the handle, he looped the strap over his head and hung the case behind his back.

Philip Knight scanned the area behind the buildings. Not a single person was afoot on Elm

Street at that hour. He hooked the handle of his tool box on a carabiner connected to his belt. Demonstrating considerable athletic ability, he grabbed on to the maintenance ladder and quickly navigated the vertical twelve feet to the roof top. He gently lowered himself onto the flat composition roof and made his way to the shade of the three-story building adjoining.

Sweat was forming in the hat band of the billed cable company hat he wore. He removed it and wiped his brow with the back of his hand. *At least I'm in the shade now. Can't believe how stinking hot that roof was in the sun.*

Knight disconnected the tool box and set it at his feet. He swung the larger black case in front of him, opened it and removed a strange looking device. The two foot long silver-colored tube resembled an oversized flashlight and had a concave six-inch metal reflector with a red lens affixed to the front. He pulled out a small piece of black injected plastic—about the size of a deck of cards—and slipped it to a tapered slot milled into the forward potion of the tube. He tightened a set-screw on the bottom of the new addition using a Leatherman tool from his belt.

Next, he added a unit fabricated from an AR-15 pistol grip and trigger to a milled slot located closer to the back. One more larger piece resembled a rifle buttstock. It had a short section of heavy insulated copper wire that terminated in a male USB connection protruding from the narrow end. Knight plugged it into a matching female receptacle in the tube body, pushed the buttstock over matching threads on the tube itself and twisted it until they locked securely in place.

Satisfied that his invention was once again operational, he set it against the building wall and opened the tool box. He carefully lifted the Steiner 3-15x56 telescopic sight from its foam bed. The scope was equipped with Leupold quick disconnect rings that mated perfectly with bases he had installed earlier on the weapon tube. He aligned the posts with the holes, dropped it into position and thumbed the levers forward to the locked position.

Philip smiled to himself as he checked his watch. *Less than one hour to payback.* He took what appeared to be a ball point pen out of his shirt pocket. Removing the cap, he exposed a micro camera lens. He grabbed his cell phone and opened an app. He twisted the head on the pen and the camera came alive—wirelessly transmitting the signal to his phone. He aimed the pen camera at himself and was pleased with the clarity of the color transmission. His hand reached for a tan block of modeling clay. The shade matched the stucco on the building below him. He bent over and moved closer to the south wall of the building.

Carefully he reached up and placed the camera pen on the three foot high brick ledge facing California Street. He monitored its video feed and tweaked the malleable clay until the west side stairwell and sidewalk were in plain view. Knight pulled his arm down and zoomed in the camera using his app. *All is well.*

Philip took a seat beside his death ray gun and leaned his back against the wall.

COOKE COUNTY COURTHOUSE

Bone forced a smile. "Aren't you glad you didn't bet me on that six pack?"

"How can you think about beer at a time like this?"

"You mean those times when I'm right? Double D, this happens all the time...or haven't you noticed?"

"Damn you, Bone...You're so..."

The sound of the doors opening to the district courtroom cut her off. She spun around to watch the first of the spectators leaving. "Dang it. We'll have to try to hold the target here."

Bone chuckled. "Have you worked with lawyers very much?"

"No, but I'm sure they'll listen to reason."

"Really? You haven't met Jimmy Jack."

"But when we tell him..."

Bone held up a hand and grinned. "They call him Diamond Head behind his back...And, sweetie pie, that ain't 'cause he likes Hawaii."

The plaintiff in the divorce action, a stunning thirty-nine year old redhead—wearing a short-skirt and tight fitting white oxford-cloth blouse—walked out of the courtroom with a smile on her face.

Her attorney was whispering to her as they passed Bone, "The judge will look favorably on my motion to force your husband to disclose all assets he had before the marriage. With a little luck, he'll have to cough up half of them as well."

"Excellent...I should have dumped Ronnie years ago," the willowy woman said. She looked up at Bone, smiled and batted her green eyes.

He said nothing, but checked her out closely as she passed—admiring her hourglass figure and tanned, toned legs.

Loraine caught his line of sight. She leaned closer to Bone and whispered in a low voice, "You have a thing for tall women?"

He nodded. "Uh huh...but it's the same thing I use on the shorter ones, too." He made a face and whispered, "Did you see all the jewelry on that chic? It would take two years of my salary to buy all that bling."

Jimmy Jack and his client were the last ones to leave the richly wood paneled room.

The forty-five year old doctor was sporting a concerned look. "She can't do that, can she? I made those investments before I even met her."

Jimmy Jack showed one of his patented smiles that reeked of insincerity. "Don't you worry about a thing, Ronnie boy. I got this under control…Trust me."

Before the defendant could respond, Bone moved in and partially blocked the way. "Pardon me, gents. We need to have a word with Jimmy."

Loraine moved to Bone's side. Her face was a study in serious concern.

Jimmy Jack looked up at Bone—a man almost a full head taller than he. "No problem, folks. I got a minute." He turned to Doctor Ron Witherspoon. "Don't fret your little head, son. We'll get it all straightened out first thing in the morning…No sweat. See you at nine sharp."

Doctor Ron left, with a look of concern on his face as well.

Jimmy waited until his client was almost to the stairwell to speak. "What's up kids? Make it quick…it's almost happy hour."

"That may be true," Bone said. "But we have something more pressing than three fingers of Laphroaig on the rocks."

"How'd you know I'm a Scotch man?"

"Lucky guess…The reason we are here is to advise you of a credible threat on your life."

BONE'S PARADOX

Jimmy Jack grinned and waved his hand. "Hell, son...Ask any divorce lawyer worth his salt if he's been threatened and he'll tell you, yes...Comes with the territory."

Loraine shook her head. "You don't understand. Somebody killed Judge Lockhart, Brittany Wilson Knight, her boyfriend Christian and just this afternoon, Carl Spears was found murdered."

"You don't say."

"We do say," Bone countered. "Evidence points to your former client, Philip Kent Knight. Plenty of motive there."

"Yeah," He nodded. "That case was a personal disappointment...Hated to lose that one, but as the saying goes, you win some and lose some...Now if you don't mind, I've got a bottle of Lafroaig Cairdeas in my office calling' my name."

"That's 103 proof...cask aged," Bone observed.

"By God, you know your whiskey, son. I'll have to have you two over for a taste when you catch the killer...Y'all excuse me, now." He turned sideways and squeezed between the two LEOs.

Loraine was astonished and looked at Bone. "What are we gonna do?"

"Told ya." He smiled and followed after Johnson. "Come on, Pard."

The three made their way down the U-shaped stairwell to the third floor. Bone glanced at his wrist watch. *Damn it, Moomer. Where are you when I need you?*

"Team Two, Team One...say your 20."

EAST CALIFORNIA STREET

"Team Two...Westbound on California coming abeam First State Bank. Figure about ninety seconds."

"That's 'bout all the time we got. Jimmy Jack's on the way down from the forth floor."

Moomer shot a quick glance over at Rick Gore. "Team Two copies. I'll hammer down." He reached up and hit the switch for the overhead red and white light bar on the Suburban as the whistle sounded of an approaching northbound freight train.

"No, dammit, not now!" Rick exclaimed as the red lights began to flash at the California Street railroad crossing only 150 yards ahead.

Moomer waited until an approaching car passed and changed lanes over the double yellow paint to pass two pickups and a tiny Smart car in the lane ahead. It was too late.

The long steel crossing bars dropped and three diesel locomotives pulling the first of 300 rail cars began to roll through the intersection.

Moomer braked the big SUV to a sliding stop. "Son of a..." He keyed the mic on the vehicle hand piece. "Team One, Team Two."

Bone and Loraine listened to the repetitive sounds of the two short blasts, one long and one short as the Santa Fe engineer sent out his obligatory warnings from the engine's horn.

"Team One is up. How many cars you looking at?"

"Can't see the end from here. Looks like they the are slowing down for a crew change here. You want us to try the Highway 82 overpass? Five minutes minimum."

Bone glanced over at Loraine.

She shrugged. "Your call."

He took in a deep breath and let it out slowly as the train's horn sounded again, echoing up and down the buildings of the old town. Bone knew Gainesville's layout like the back of his hand. The north-south rail lines cut the town basically in half. One long train could, and often did, block every single grade level crossing at once. To further the traffic aggravation, the city served as a crew base for the railroad and also had a switching yard with six parallel sets of tracks.

"Did I ever tell you that I hate trains?" He grinned as he reached for his transmitter. "Team Two...try the overpass...Call for any available backup west of the tracks. Appreciate the try, amigo, but you can't help us...We're on our own."

§

CHAPTER NINETEEN

COOKE COUNTY COURT HOUSE

Bone opened the glass door and stepped outside into the bright Texas sunshine. He casually slipped the mirrored sunglasses on and sucked his hat down as Jimmy Jack and Loraine walked out behind him.

He could sense an evil presence, but not pick up a direction. His right hand draped over the rubber combat grip on his 500 Smith & Wesson as his thumb unfastened the nickel-plated retainer snap. In his left hand, he palmed his favorite 3"x5" pocket mirror.

Jimmy Jack slipped his French designer sun glasses on and then transferred the heavy alligator-skin brief case to his right hand.

While Bone led off in the point position, Loraine followed close behind the sixty-year old barrister, as the team had briefed back at the station. Her dark eyes darted left and right scanning every face coming up the outside steps, and then scrutinizing the surrounding rooftops—inch by inch.

She felt her pulse quicken as they descended the last step and turned north toward Jimmy Jack Johnson's law office—located across California Street from the county court house.

From his lofty vantage point, Philip Knight could watch the entire trip on his cell phone. In fact, Jimmy Jack's office was directly underneath him, two floors below. *The big dumb cop investigator is gettin' in the way. Stupid fool is blocking my shot. What's a little collateral damage in my perfect plan?* He pressed a button on the left side of the ray gun and it began to emit an almost inaudible hum as the capacitors began to charge.

Bone and the others closed the distance to fifty yards. His eyes scanned every face in every passing car and swept the doorways of the offices, restaurants and storefronts across the street. He could feel his heart rate picking up as the adrenaline kicked in.

Knight turned his hat around, shouldered the weapon and stood up near the wall. He instantly found the man-mountain wearing a cowboy hat in his crosshairs and aimed for the big man's head. He squeezed the trigger.

Bone felt an intense burning sensation in his ears. He detected movement on the rooftop across the street and drew his hand cannon like a diamondback rattler striking.

He lunged left, crouching as he yelled, "Gun!...Gun." Bone extended both hands in front of him.

Loraine rushed forward and knocked Jimmy Jack down between a pair of parked cars—simultaneously drawing her Kimber, as she searched for the shooter. Across the street, on the roof, she spotted a man wearing oversized red glasses and holding a strange looking object that appeared to be a rifle of some sort.

Bone's fifty cal fired, echoing in the concrete canyon like a howitzer.

Time seemed to stand still for Bone. He brought the small mirror directly in front of his left eye as he lined up the sights of his huge pistol with his right—the man wearing red sunglasses got a taste of his own medicine for a brief moment.

The reflected, extremely low frequency sonic stream, riding on an intense ruby red light beam began to fry his prefrontal cortex. He body started to shake, but the ray gun's deadly transmission was cut short.

A 275 grain solid cooper hollowpoint center-punched the concave light reflector and continued up the tube. It tore off the lithium gel battery pack and ripped into Knight's right shoulder.

Loraine fired two shots in rapid succession—so quickly the report was almost a single sound. A hollowpoint .45 slug smashed into his collarbone. Another removed the bottom of his left earlobe.

Knight's grip on the weapon was lost completely when a second .50 cal round punched through his larynx and demolished two vertebra as it exploded out the back of his neck. His body slumped forward over the stucco and brick parapet and tumbled to the sidewalk, nearly thirty feet below.

Loraine checked to see how Jimmy Jack was fairing. The terrified attorney was cowering behind the wheel well of one of the judges' cars.

She finally remembered to breathe and looked forward toward her partner. His knees buckled and the huge stainless steel revolver slipped from his grip and clattered to the concrete. Bone fell forward—first onto his knees and then almost face planting as he managed to catch himself on his elbows.

She screamed, "Bone! No!...No!"

The big man lost his beloved Stetson. It rolled off his head and ended upside down on the well trimmed Fescue lawn lining the sidewalk.

Loraine sprinted up to him and knelt down beside him as she put her arm around his broad shoulders. "Bone! Talk to me...where does it hurt?"

He shook his head and fought to refocus his eyes and he turned to face her. "Did we get him?"

"Oh, yeah…" She glanced across the street at the crumpled body on the sidewalk. "We double teamed his ass…Are you okay?"

"Dunno. My ears burn like hell." He put a hand to his face. "Ah…Feels like a killer sunburn."

Loraine pulled him up to a kneeling position and placed both of her hands on the sides of his face. "Tell me how Lucy does her thing."

"Focus all your energy to your hands…visualize it flowing into me.…Kinda helps if you close your eyes."

She closed her brown eyes tightly and concentrated as hard as she could—a faint blue light glowed in her palms for a few seconds then went out. Loraine felt a little woozy. "Did that do anything?"

Bone took in a deep breath and let it out. He wiped his parched lips with the back of his hand. "Believe it did…Thanks, Pard. I owe you." Bone rocked back on his heels.

She reached for his hat. Loraine noticed that the straw Stetson was abnormally heavy when she picked it up. She spotted the hammered gold foil-like liner inside the moist sweatband and up to the crown. "What this? Some sort of clandestine alien armor?"

"In a way...I think it kept old Phil over there from scamblin' my brains."

She glanced back to the body lying across the street. "Is that real gold?"

"Uh-huh...Hammered it out it from part of Lucy's stash of gold bars she gave us when I couldn't sleep last night."

Loraine heard the sound of at least two sirens approaching from the north. "Here comes the cavalry."

Bone laughed. "Where's a cop when you need one?"

§

EPILOGUE

GAINESVILLE POLICE DEPARTMENT

Bone studied the remains of Philip Knight's death ray gun. "You know, between the round pulverizin' the innards and the perpetrator's body landing on this weird sucker, I'm not certain we'll ever figure out how it worked."

Loraine smiled. "I'm not so sure that's a bad thing…It nearly killed you, you big ox."

Bone grinned. "That takes a heap a doin', I'm happy to report."

"You sure you're ready to get back to work? The captain said to take a week off…Only been four days."

"I can still count…Got bored out there at the ranch. Have to get Stella's exculpatory evidence ready for the grand jury. Besides, knowing you had all these reports to get out by yourself, it didn't seem fair."

"Thank you, kind sir. There may be help for you after all."

Bone began to place the remains of the enigmatic weapon in a plain cardboard box. He wrapped yellow adhesive tape on the top seams emblazoned with the words *EVIDENCE*, in large black letters. Once that was done, he affixed a preprinted sticker with the case number, date and his signature on the side of the box.

Captain St. John entered the office without knocking. He had a pair of FedEx boxes in his hands.

"Hey, Cap'n. I see they found a job you can cross train into."

"Very funny, wise guy. I've half a mind to keep these for myself."

"I remember when you lost the other half...A day that will go down in infamy." Bone grinned.

Loraine gave him a *cut it out* hand signal.

St. John glared at him. "Honestly..." He shook his head. "Looks like you guys impressed Jimmy Jack Johnson when you saved his hardheaded butt. Here's one for each of you."

The longer lighter package went to Loraine. Bone's was not as long, but weighed more.

"What did he send?" Loraine asked.

St. John shook his head. "Madam...I am totally aclueistic. You'll have to open it to see. I just was up front and signed for these when the delivery was made."

Bone fished in his pocket for his Case Trapper and slit the packaging open on one end. He looked across the aisle. "Hey, Pard. Need a knife?"

She was fumbling with the super-strong adhesive on the packaging. "Uh-huh."

He closed the blade and tossed it to her. She caught it gracefully.

220

BONE'S PARADOX

"Thanks...Didn't want to break a nail." She pried out the clip point back and slit the end of the packaging. Another rectangular box with a plastic see-though cover was inside. It contained a dozen long-stem red roses and a simple note:

To my beautiful guardian angel,
I am forever in your debt.
Jimmy Jack

Loraine's eyes misted over. "Aw."

Bone ripped the end off of his package. He tilted the box up and another box, much more ornate, slid out. He turned it over to read the label.

LAFROAIG CAIDEAS
CASK AGED
TEN YEARS

"Holy crap! This stuff is over $300 a bottle."

St. John smiled. "Don't drop it, hammer hands. I hate to see a grown man cry."

"Not a chance." He cradled it in his arms like a baby.

"What does the card say, Bone?" Loraine asked.

221

"Gimme chance, girl." He laid the bottle on his desk, found the card loose in the outer box and tilted it to drop it free. He jammed an index finger under the flap and lifted it up. The card inside was embossed print on fine linen stationary.

The message was short:

To my white knight in shinning armor:
Your bravery is a thing of legend.
Your Humble Servant,
Jimmy Jack Johnson
Aka
Diamond Head

Bone burst into a deep belly laugh.

Shortly before 3 AM, a shadowy figure clothed entirely in black made its way down the darkened halls of the police station. Wearing night vision goggles, he approached the evidence room and held up a small electronic device to the magnetic card reader. The light on the lock turned green, and he silently turned the door knob and made his way inside. He closed the door behind him without making a sound.

Using an IR illuminator, he navigated the row upon row of evidence until he found the item he sought. He used a razor sharp auto opening knife to slice a single thin cut in the evidence tape sealing the top of the box. He carefully removed the remains of Philip Knight's most nefarious invention and dropped them into a long black cloth sack hooked to a D ring on his belt. He closed the sack securely and reached into the tactical vest he wore to remove a roll of yellow and black evidence tape.

He folded the top of the cardboard box closed and expertly aligned the new tape with that which he had sliced. He slid a gloved hand over the shiny adhesive backed sealant and placed the box back on the shelf exactly like he had found it.

In less than a minute the figure departed the back door of the station and disappeared into the stillness of the dark night.

§§§

PREVIEW
OF
THE NEXT EXCITING

BUCK STIENKE NOVEL

NO TIME TO DIE

CHAPTER ONE

NORTHEAST ARKANSAS

July 15, 1863

"Light the fuses boys…that Yankee train will be here in thirty seconds," the lanky Confederate lieutenant colonel ordered.

He backed the spirited lineback dun stallion away from the elevated roadbed and into the towering loblolly pines that lined both sides of the remote section of track.

"You got it, Colonel," replied the master sergeant who had supervised the laying of the black powder charges.

Four enlisted men scratched the wooden lucifers they carried against the shiny polished top surface of the steel rails—phosphorous and sulfur responded to the friction and burst into flame as the nervous soldiers touched them to the intentionally frayed ends of the identical fuses.

Each lit off with a continuous hiss that sounded like an angry rattlesnake preparing to strike, complete with a small tendril of smoke that curled up in the humid still air. They sprinted to their horses being held by other members of the Second Battalion of Texas Cavalry, grabbed the reins and mounted up without delay.

Each knew the total of thirty-two pounds of explosives buried under the rails would be more than enough to do what the planner of the military expedition had in mind. None of them wanted to become a casualty from flying debris. They wheeled about and rode into the woods on the inside of the gradual turn and waited.

As the summer sun set, the engineer in the Union Army troop train checked his pocket watch. The fancy gold timepiece—complete with an embossed image of the 6-4-2 wood-fired steam engine that pulled the twelve cars—indicated it was almost 7 PM. *Looks like another on-time arrival in Little Rock.* He wound the stem six times and dropped the fancy gift from the railroad president back into his bib overalls.

Elliott R. Patterson was a dedicated company man. Fourteen years on the job and he had never had an accident. His on-time record was second to none in the company and this milk run from Saint Louis to Little Rock was like so many others he had made. Coming down the steep grade in the Ozarks, he had pulled off a little on the power, letting gravity do the work. He knew the tracks leveled off as they came out of the turn to the west and nudged the Johnson bar forward a bit.

He checked the gauge on the boiler and saw what his ears had already told him. The increased power demand he asked for was being transferred to the pistons working furiously beneath the deck of the glistening black cab.

The essentially coasting train began to pick up even more speed under its own power as he called out to his fireman, "Willis, feed this big boy if we are ever gonna make it to the station on time."

"Break time's over, I reckon." The thirty-five year old native of Indiana wiped his damp brow with red and blue paisley print bandana and stuffed it in his back pocket of his faded overalls.

The midsummer temperature didn't need any help at all from the engine's firebox to make a man break into a sweat. He used a hooked poker to lift the latch on the thick cast iron door and chunked a few pieces of seasoned oak into the hellish compartment.

Temperatures in the engine cab rose to 140 degrees for a few seconds before he slammed the door closed and flipped the latch back into place. "There you go, ER...Does that make you a happy man?"

Patterson nodded and lit a carved cherry wood pipe and drew in a deep breath of the pungent smelling tobacco as the rails ahead curved gracefully westward. He exhaled a plume of blue-gray smoke into the fifty miles per hour breeze whistling past the cab and squinted as the golden rays of the setting sun reflected of the twin ribbons of steel. He blinked his eyes twice and pulled his head back inside, trying to readjust his vision from the temporary sun blindness.

One fuse set off its eight pound charge a full second before the others. A joint where two sections of track were attached was blasted upward, twisted and separated by over a foot. Captain Doran Ingrham cursed the early detonation—a full eighty yards in front of the train's cowcatcher.

He needn't have worried, as the relatively heavy train would have taken a quarter mile to slow to a stop under the best of circumstances. As he watched, the other blasts thundered their way through the roadbed and sent splinters and chunks of burning creosote-soaked railroad ties up into the undercarriage of the engine's wood tender, two passenger cars and the third freight car.

Without the outer rail in place to hold the train to the curve, the centrifugal force of the train cars forced them to drop off the inner rail as well. One by one, they began to tilt as they derailed, sending showers of crushed limestone rocks flying off the rapidly spinning cast iron wheels. The coupling between the engine and tender released and the fully laden car tipped over, dumping its top-heavy load of firewood as it barreled into the trees with a mighty crash that reverberated through the forest.

ER Patterson yanked back on the Johnson bar and hit the brakes, instantly locking the drive wheels on Engine number 29 with a high-pitched screech that could be heard for miles.

One second later, the shiny pride of the Union Pacific railroad crossed over the torn apart rail joint and vaulted off the five foot high roadbed into the waist deep brush that had grown alongside the track.

He and his fireman screamed as the engine plowed though the underbrush and careened into the woods—landing upright and continued barreling into the forest as the cast iron cowcatcher caromed off of some four foot thick trees and snapped off other smaller ones with impunity.

Union soldiers riding in the passengers cars had been playing cards, chatting up one another with war stories of real and imagined heroism from their battles in the never-ending war. However, as the flimsy cars accordioned into each other, crushed and twisted in all directions in the blink of an eye, the only sounds that could be heard above the tortured tune of agonized metal shearing and wood splintering were the cries of men and boys screaming out in stark terror and pain.

Damnation...worked better than I thought it would. Lt. Colonel Eric Schmidt mused as he watched the mayhem that his surprise attack on the enemy troop train had created. He pulled the double barreled muzzle loading shotgun from it custom-made leather scabbard—an accouterment years ahead of its time—hand crafted by his late father.

"Bugler, sound the attack!"

The young corporal from Tyler blew the notes for the nearly three hundred men to initiate their charge. The signal was repeated by two other company buglers and followed almost immediately with a chorus of rebel yells designed to instill fear in the enemy. The impassioned blood curling yelps—reminiscent of several bands of coyotes howling— worked.

Most of the survivors of the train wreck opted to give up to the hordes of gray clad cavalrymen that descended upon them like vengeful locusts. Others who dared to bring weapons to bear on the volunteers from Texas fell in a furious fuselage of pistol and rifle fire at close range.

Eric tapped his heels to Bucky's ribs, urging the dun to break from the safety of the dark timber and lope up and across the roadbed. He reined him right to clear the cloud of steam venting from the boiler, seam where a missing row of rivets told of an unanticipated steel plate flexing caused by the derailment. *Good thing. The last thing we need is a steam explosion while we check this wreck for supplies.*

The Union naval blockade of the Mississippi and the ports all along the Gulf coast had left the Confederacy woefully short of necessities. Intercepting enemy supply wagons, trains and barges was one way to try to tip the scales.

Movement at the back of the engine caught his attention. A man wearing faded blue overalls staggered to the platform and held on to his midsection. It was obvious he was in pain from some unseen injury.

Willis caught sight of the Confederate officer holding a shotgun leveled at him and raised his hands up—away from the second degree burns that he suffered when he had been thrown forward against the closed firebox door during the crash. The soldier motioned for him to step down and he readily complied.

Schmidt waved him to continue back toward the rest of the cars and didn't catch the sight of the second man peeking around the door frame at the back of the cab until it was too late.

The engineer's hat was missing and a fresh gash above his eyes spoke of his harsh contact with some hard object. Blood ran down his nose and dripped across the front of his overalls, but that didn't stop him from pulling a Colt .36 caliber pistol from his left rear pocket and taking a shot at the mounted rebel commander.

Eric wheeled the scattergun around and fired as the railroad man pulled the trigger. The two shots rang out as one, with acrid sulfurous gunsmoke belching out in both directions. The load of 00 buckshot lifted Patterson off his feet and sprayed his brains across the rear of his beloved Engine number 29. His body slide backwards off the platform and disappeared on the far side.

"Colonel! You all right?" shouted one of his senior NCOs.

"Yeah…Lucky for me he could not shoot worth a…"

His reply was cut short as his mount took a couple of steps backwards and then lurched to the side. *Oh my God…Bucky.* He released the reins and swung his right leg over the high cantle of his McClellen saddle and hopped out of the left stirrup on to the rock strewn side of the tracks.

Keeping one hand on his horse, he eased around the front to see a small hole in the buckskin's chest. Frothy bright red bubbles dripped from its nose and a thin streak of crimson ran down between his legs. Bucky's eyes were wide with fear as he tried to process what ailment have befallen him.

"Easy boy, take it easy," he said as he stroked the stallion's neck. "You gotta calm down, Bucky. Everything is gonna be…"

The magnificent horse's knees buckled as it eyes rolled back. Eric tried to hold him up, but there was nothing anyone could have done. Shot though the aorta, his much loved horse had died as a cavalryman's mount in combat.

The twenty-one year old soldier was devastated. He had treasured the animal for ten years, ever since its birth and never owned another. Tears rimmed his eyes as his first sergeant dismounted and stepped closer.

"Colonel...sir, we got things to do, sir...I will have one of the men strip your gear and have a replacement mount brought up."

Eric wiped back the tears with the back of his gloved hand as he got to his feet. "Do that, Sergeant Major. Take that man into custody," he said pointing at the injured fireman. "See to his wounds."

He lay the shotgun down beside his fallen horse and drew a Remington .44 caliber sixgun from his hip. Turning back toward the wrecked engine, he strode off purposefully.

Sporadic gunfire had almost dissipated when he reached the back of the still steaming engine and cautiously looked around the far side. The engineer's body was lying upside down on the steps up to the platform. Beside him lay the Colt revolver.

Eric picked up the six shooter and slipped it under his uniform belt. He took one last look at the what remained of the face of the man that had tried to kill him. Schmidt burned the image into his memory. *You sorry dumb bastard...You just could not leave well enough alone, could you?*

He started to turn away, but the glint of a flash of gold from the front of the man's overalls caught his attention. Eric reached down and withdrew a gold timepiece, complete with a solid gold chain. He examined the embossed cover and then turned it over to read the short inscription engraved on the back.

To ER Patterson
For long and faithful service.

He tucked the watch into his tunic and looked at the sightless brown eyes staring back up at him. *Nowhere near enough an even trade for my Bucky, but I reckon it is all you had.*

Eric looked back to the wreckage of the train where his men had Union soldiers crawling out of the demolished cars with their hands up. Several were being relieved of their sidearms. He took in a deep breath and let it out slowly.

§§§

OTHER NOVELS FROM
TIMBER CREEK PRESS
www.timbercreekpress.net

MILITARY ACTION/TECHNO
BLACK EAGLE FORCE: Eye of the Storm (Book #1)
by Buck Stienke and Ken Farmer
BLACK EAGLE FORCE: Sacred Mountain (Book #2) by Buck Stienke and Ken Farmer
RETURN of the STARFIGHTER (Book #3)
by Buck Stienke and Ken Farmer
BLACK EAGLE FORCE: BLOOD IVORY (Book #4)
by Buck Stienke and Ken Farmer with Doran Ingrham
BLACK EAGLE FORCE: FOURTH REICH (Book #5) by Buck Stienke and Ken Farmer
AURORA: INVASION (Book #6 in the BEF) by Ken Farmer & Buck Stienke
BLACK EAGLE FORCE: ISIS (Book #7) by Buck Stienke and Ken Farmer
BLOOD BROTHERS - Doran Ingrham, Buck Stienke and Ken Farmer
DARK SECRET - Doran Ingrham
NICARAGUAN HELL - Doran Ingrham
BLACKSTAR BOMBER by T.C. Miller

BLACKSTAR BAY by T.C. Miller
BLACKSTAR MOUNTAIN by T.C. Miller

HISTORICAL FICTION WESTERN
THE NATIONS by Ken Farmer and Buck Stienke
HAUNTED FALLS by Ken Farmer and Buck Stienke
HELL HOLE by Ken Farmer
ACROSS the RED by Ken Farmer and Buck Stienke
BASS and the LADY by Ken Farmer and Buck Stienke
DEVIL'S CANYON by Buck Stienke
LADY LAW by Ken Farmer
BLUE WATER WOMAN by Ken Farmer
FLYNN by Ken Farmer
AURALI RED by Ken Farmer
COLDIRON by Ken Farmer
STEELDUST by Ken Farmer
BONE by Ken Farmer
BONE'S LAW by Ken Farmer
BONE & LORAINE by Ken Farmer
BONE'S GOLD by Ken Farmer

SY/FY
LEGEND of AURORA by Ken Farmer & Buck
Stienke
AURORA: INVASION (Book #6 in the BEF) by
Ken Farmer & Buck Stienke

HISTORICAL FICTION ROMANCE
THE TEMPLAR TRILOGY
MYSTERIOUS TEMPLAR by Adriana Girolami
THE CRIMSON AMULET by Adriana Girolami
TEMPLAR'S REDEMPTION by Adriana Girolami

Coming Soon

HISTORICAL FICTION WESTERN
NO TIME to DIE by Buck Stienke (sequel to
Devil's Canyon by Buck Stienke
BONE'S ENIGMA by Ken Farmer

HISTORICAL FICTION ROMANCE
DAUGHTER of HADES by Adriana Girolami
ZAMINDAR and the LADY by Adriana Girolami
MILITARY ACTION/TECHNO
BLACKSTAR RANCH by T.C. Miller

SY/FY
ANTAREAN DILEMMA by T.C. Miller

Thanks for reading *BONE'S PARADOX*. If you enjoyed it, I would really appreciate a review on Amazon. My Author Page is:
www.amazon.com/Buck-Stienke/e/B0057XZNKW
Email - buckstienke@yahoo.com

Personally autographed books available at our web site:
Web page: www.timbercreekpress.net

TIMBER CREEK PRESS